Doing Life with Hope

ISBN:979-8-9889305-3-2 - Softcover Edition

Published December 2023
Printed in the United States of America

For information about this title or to order books and/or electronic media, contact the publisher:
Sula Too Publishing
www.sulatoo.com/publishing

Doing Life with Hope

A Patchwork Journey

Novel by
Ingrid Landis-Davis

Sula Too Publishing

Contents

Prologue - Bridge

The road to Trinity is long, steep, and winding. Wintu Indian, Three-Finger Jack, knew that old Anderson, the white man he was stalking, would have to pass within his vantage point, atop Bully Choop peak. When Anderson rounded into view on his big spotted mule, Three-Finger Jack jumped on his sorrel and rode low along the ridgeline.

He would follow him until he found the best spot to take his revenge. For indeed, it was Anderson who had given Three-Finger Jack the famous moniker when he was young, by cutting off two of his digits for stealing.

If the white men had not muddied up the rivers looking for the yellow sand, the native fumed; there would not have been a need to steal food. The Wintu had always had a plentiful supply of fish and game. Since the miners arrived, they could barely feed their women and children through the winter.

Rays of sunlight chased shadows across the high valley floor and clouds rapidly passed overhead. Dogwoods blossomed in the gulches and tall Ponderosa Pines reached for the sky on the mountain ridge leading to Chanchellulla Peak. The watercourse, known as Bridge Gulch, bubbled, and rapidly flowed over smooth stream rocks and large outcroppings. As he descended into the narrow valley, Three-Finger Jack observed this beauty with the swelling pride of ownership. He set up his ambush for Anderson in a narrow curve where the trail was hugged by high rocks and overshadowed by bushy Sugar Pines. Here, Hay Fork Creek, the lower stream, flowed rapidly toward the path and, after the winter thaw, overran its banks leaving large round stones that had to be cleared away in late spring for passage. It was rough going for the mule and Three-Fingered Jack knew that Anderson would be concentrating on making his way through the area. The ambush spot was near the fork for The Natural Bridge.

The Natural Bridge, a large limestone outcropping that the water course had eroded a tunnel through, soon came into view. As Anderson wound carefully around the sharp bend, Three-Finger Jack sprang from his hiding place on the rocks above the trail. In a quick swoop he reached under the mule with a large knife cut the saddle ties and pushed Anderson right off the mule. Before Anderson could even get to his gun, he was dragged off his mount saddle, stabbed, and scalped.

As the mule ran away, Three-Finger Jack knew he'd made a tactical mistake, that mule knew his way home from anywhere in these mountains. The riderless animal would give away the fact that Anderson was not still away on the trail taking care of his business.

Three-Finger Jack did not care as he whooped and hollered holding Anderson's scalp aloft and waving it to the sky. His enemy was dead. He reached into his pouch, took out some firewater and swigged deeply several times in celebration. He moved the body behind a log off the trail, threw the saddle into forest bushes and removed all signs of his tracks. He headed back deep into the upper mountains to his hideaway.

Little Buck kept himself very still as he watched Three-Finger Jack attack the white man and hide his body. He knew his parents would not approve of his leaving the sacred camp. He had felt adventurous, and impatient to get the high ceremonies that would initiate him into manhood started. The elders, however, were taking their sweet time, in the sweathouse *hlut*, passing the pipe and discussing the characteristics of each of the boys participating in the ceremonies. Little Buck managed to sneak out.

He'd spent some time crawling through some of the caves and was heading back to camp when he saw Three-Finger Jack creeping among the rocks.

Little Buck was astonished at what he'd witnessed. The Wintu did not make war with the white man, if they could help it, and certainly not near the sacred place of the Natural Bridge. He watched the crazy man carefully lead his horse away, then he headed toward the camp to tell his father this awful news.

Little Buck started off running at a good clip. He stumbled over a heavy object hidden in grass on the path. It was the white man's saddle bags that had fallen off his bolting mule. Little Buck lifted it to throw it further into bush. It was too heavy. He opened it and examined the contents. There were several large pouches of yellow sand and some sacks of yellow rocks. Little Buck knew that the white men placed a high value on this "gold". He didn't know what to do about it. If he was found with it, they might think his Nor-Rel-Muk people had something to do with that old man's death.

After a second of thought, he decided to bury the bags someplace near the caves. He could use the rocks there to quickly cover them. He knew he would need to hurry because his parents might soon notice that he was not with the other older boys who were to be initiated today. Little Buck would seek his father's wisdom on this after the ceremony, for he did not want anything to ruin the festivities. He buried the saddle bags and arrived back at the sacred camp just as his father was looking for him to join the men in the sweat lodge.

The Rite of Manhood passage was very solemn, although there was much dancing and singing. The Wintu did not use grueling physical tests of strength for these rites. Instead, the chief and elders provided lengthy counseling to determine the character of each boy so that their birth names could be formally changed to better suit their destiny.

Little Buck had felt distracted even haunted during the rituals, however afterwards he was very proud of his new name, which was now White Wolf. He knew that this rare spirit would protect him at all times. It was late evening, the moon had already set, before he could take his father aside and tell him what Three-

Finger Jack had done to the white man and about the yellow sand. His father was very tired because the men had been preparing for the rites for two days, but he went to the chief's fire and spoke in quiet tones to him about the matter.

Chief Pentallis, White Wolf's mother's father, listened with growing concern. His grandfather called the boy by his new name, White Wolf; had him sit at his side and repeat the story of the murder of the white man. His grandfather waved a special blessing over him and declared that someday White Wolf would make a great Chief of the Trinity for he had the vigilance and stealth of his new namesake. White Wolf knew he had made his father proud even though he was not supposed to be out of the camp at the time. His powerful Spirit had protected him.

Word was passed that a decision had been made to break camp and leave the Natural Bridge at early light. No one questioned it, knowing that a decision of this type would have something to do with white men. They usually spent most of the summer at the sacred camp, enjoying the cool grottos and soothing stream.

White Wolf's father told him to go get the saddle bags before first light so as not to leave such an unholy thing at the sacred place. He tossed and turned on his pallet for an hour or two until he saw the morning star. He rose quietly, made his roll, slipped through the slumbering camp, and headed for the sacred caves to get the saddle bag. He would not need to help his mother break camp now that he was an initiated buck, for that was women's work. It kind of made him sad because he loved working with his mother who knew many things about nature and taught them to him in a soft, gentle voice.

It was still pre-dawn when White Wolf arrived at the caves. He sat down to his breakfast of hard tack. He knew he would have to wait until first light to see well enough to dig up the bags. He spent the waiting time pulling on his tack, going over the previous evening's ceremony and thinking of his grandfather's later declaration over him.

As soon as the sky brightened a little, he went into the mouth of the cave and found the pile of rocks that he'd used to cover the saddlebag. He ran out of the cave when he thought he heard a gunshot. Then all hell broke loose. He heard gunfire echoing all around the valley, screams from the sacred camp, and horses neighing in fear. White Wolf's first instinct was to run to his parents at the camp. He was stopped in his tracks when he thought he heard his mother's gentle voice say, "Wait!"

White Wolf crept through the brush closer to the camp, he knew the white men were shooting at his people, but he was unprepared for the massacre that he saw there.

Everyone, children included, was dead or dying and all the summer lodges were afire. White Wolf knew this was the end of the Nor- Rel-Muk unless he could escape. Back at the cave, White Wolf vowed his revenge. He laid low until dusk. He'd had no time to dig up the saddlebags before the white men came, so he piled more markings on them.

White Wolf left the cave at dark. He intended to make his way down to Cottonwood Creek to the summer camp of his father's people, but in his grief and desire to avoid the miners or sheriff's people, he took a very roundabout way and headed up into Wildwood mountain.

After weeks of careful climbing and backtracking, he came to his father's people's camp. There he told the tale of the murder of the white man by Three-Finger Jack, the finding of the saddlebags, his grandfather's declaration and finally the massacre of the Nor-Rel- Muk.

The telling took a long time for every family killed had to be named, for the proper wailing by the women, at least two hundred or more souls were lost. The Chief's council decided that the white men had attacked because of the missing white man and his yellow sand. For his safety, they sent the boy further south to another Wintu group in the valley.

White Wolf grew to a fine man in the south. He always desired in his heart to get his revenge on Sheriff Dixon for the massacre of his family. A few years later, he followed the mountain trail up to the South Fork and wended his way towards the Natural Bridge, even though, the experience caused his heart to seize in terror from the long-ago night that his family died there. He was camped at the stream fork, when suddenly, a man was by his side. He had not heard his approach, as he was exhausted and hungry. He had eaten only the wild raspberries that he'd found along the trails.

"Do not be frightened," the man spoke to him in White Wolf's own language.

"I know some of your people," he said in answer to White Wolf's astonishment at his speaking in his tongue.

"Who are you?" White Wolf asked, for he was not a white man. He was not a Wintu either. White Wolf wondered if perhaps he was some sort of woods spirit for his skin was a dark red and although his hair was long, it was tangled and coarse.

But the man answered, "My name is Skinner, some people call me Mule. I'm part Cherokee, some call me a Blackfoot. My people are from east of the great river. I am what some people call a Buffalo Soldier. Sometimes I track and scout for the white man. I know what was done to your family at your sacred summer camp for it has been talked of for many years by the white folks here."

White Wolf recoiled from the man, "They killed everyone… including my mother….the women……the babies. How could they and all for the yellow sand? I will have my revenge on them sooner or later. Are you here to kill me now ……the last of my father's seed?"

"No, no, no! Let me help you, though. You can't survive on this mountain alone with the miners running around everywhere and often, some of them have blood on their minds. What is your name?"
White Wolf drew his tired shoulders back and looked at Skinner

with pride and gave his name, "My name is White Wolf, the eldest son of Iron Hand and Nuya-Pokta, grandson of Pentallis, Chief of the Trinity Nor-Rel-Muk Wintu."

Skinner regarded him solemnly, "I will help you White Wolf and you need not repay me for it is I who owe you, for I have come to your land to live. Now you are tired and weak with grief. I invite you to my camp on the valley side of Dubakella Mountain.

The white men have not yet settled on that side of the mountain… no yellow sand found there. You must gather your strength for the path you have chosen."

"I have buried yellow sand in the caves. I will give it to you for your help as I seek my revenge," White Wolf later told Mule Skinner. Skinner just shook his head and told the man that he did not want blood money and the white man would just take any yellow sand that he tried to trade at market, anyway.

Later, after they had slipped into town, White Wolf cut a few specific throats, Skinner helped him escape back down the mountain. It was never discovered who did it.

Chapter 1

Chiefs of the Trinity

Eureka!

Standing over the clutching dead body, with the fiery dawn warming his face, Carpenter knew that he'd steal the gold. It was blood money, but his workingman's life had chewed him up then spewed him out into this meager path of day labor. This was his chance to take back the pound of flesh he'd exchanged for the pennies they'd given.

Carpenter stroked his long unruly beard as he tried to figure out how to get away from here. He was driving the Dubakella Mountain Fire Department's water tank and deployed to bring back water from the nearest pond to the staging area. The wild forest fire had roared all night and he had been called in by his ex-wife as a relief driver. She had insisted that he keep his credentials in order, even though, he'd left the department when she'd been named Assistant Fire Chief.

Truth be told, it was the final straw that broke the back of their marriage. Here he was a man with three strapping sons and his wife gets promoted over him. He'd had enough of the insults. Women were running way too many things for his taste. He still couldn't figure out how that woman Hope Morlan got elected Fire Chief. She was the only black woman in the whole county and what she knew about firefighting, humph, he could put in a bottle and drink it up in one swallow. They said they needed a good organizer, administrator and grant writer who could ferret out the budgets. Well, they got that, she was as by the book as they come.

Plus, she was constantly having her community "outreach" and "educational" meetings that seemed to him to consist mostly of her and the other women showing off their culinary skills.

Chief Hope's saying was, "It's not about race or money; it's about community."

There was always food galore at the meetings which was why so many folks came out. He shook himself back to the problem at hand, getting the gold and himself away from the fire scene. He had to work fast because he did not want to have to explain the dead firefighter. Getting out of a fire staging area wasn't as easy as it sounded. When you are deployed to drive equipment, the procedure is that the Chief or Commander in charge of the staging, needs to know where you and the equipment are at all times.

At this point, he was about to break all the rules. It went against his rather formidable training. He didn't care. He didn't want any trouble with the law, but he wanted that gold. If he reported the dead body, the sheriff would, at the very least, want to question him and more than likely be suspicious of anything he had to say.

He picked up the thick leather saddlebags from the body, haul-tailed it to the tanker and maneuvered the heavy truck down the dirt road toward the highway. He'd speed pass the staging area, back to the Dubakella Mountain Fire Hall where he'd left his own truck, go home, lock his gate, and not answer his phone. Nobody would dare come on his property without a warrant. He had warning signs everywhere. His ex, Joanie, was too busy with her duties on the fire to come after him at this point. It would give him a chance to get home and figure out what to do to protect the gold.

He knew eventually he would have to answer for leaving the fire scene with fire fighting apparatus without following proper procedure. However, he had to protect the gold first and figure out how to field questions later. Since there would likely be a formal hearing, he probably had plenty of time to find something plausible to throw off the Fire Chiefs. Of course, the dead firefighter would add a crick to things, but there was nothing he could do about that.

With spittle entangled and freezing in his chest-length, wiry gray beard, nothing showing out from under his knit cap, but his cracked eyeglasses and hooked nose, the old man was a vision of kinetic energy. Waving his shovel in the air, his spindly thin legs slipping and sliding on ice patches, he ran towards the approaching snowplow.

"Look out, Snapp!" The rider shouted at the driver, when he espied the man running down the long driveway, directly at them. "Here comes that crazy Carpenter guy. He's getting in front of the plow!"

The lumbering truck skidded to a complete halt, as the man laid down on the snowy gravel road in front of the plow blade. The driver and the rider looked at each other and sighed in exasperation.

"Somabitch!" Snapp said as he banged his large, beefy hand on the big steering wheel, "What should we do?"

"You stay in the truck, keep the engine running. Be prepared to take off if I give you the signal." the rider said, opening the truck door and climbing down.

"He doesn't really know me so maybe I can reason with him."

He approached the prostrate man gingerly. "What's the matter here?" he asked.

"Why you pushing those berms in my driveway? I just shoveled it," the old man screamed without moving. "You don't need to plow this road anyway. I'm the only one living on it. Did I ask you to plow it?"

"Carpenter, this is my first time helping to plow these roads. With this early snow, we're just getting used to this old snowplow again," he patted the top of the blade gingerly as he spoke. "You've driven it before. You know you have to baby it along."

"Yeah, I've driven it before and I didn't block people's driveway with snow berms," Carpenter allowed from his prone position on the icy ground.

"Well, we'll try to fix that. Why don't you let us do our job and we'll try to clear your driveway, okay? At least this early snow help put out the wildfire"

He reached out a hand amiably to help the man to his feet. Carpenter starred at him a second and after a moment, he got up, ignoring the outstretched hand of the other guy, saying in a plaintive voice, "I don't want that Snapp fella on my property. He's a bum and a thief. I'm too old to have to keep shoveling out this driveway so that I can drive my truck out."

The other man said, as he eased toward the passenger door of the plow, "Well, none of us in these hills are getting any younger. How old are you, anyway?"

Carpenter glared at him suspiciously, backed away and replied in a threatening tone, "Old enough to protect my money!"

The other man laughed as he made a secret signal to Snapp to put the plow in gear. The big old International diesel jumped forward, as he grabbed the large steel mirror bar and stepped up on to the sideboard. He was still laughing as the truck lumbered down the road leaving Carpenter standing there waving his shovel and yelling obscenities after them.

That's where Joanie found him as she muscled the snowmobile around the sharp bend onto Carpenter's road. Bare headed, her thick, naturally blond, wavy, waist-length mane flowed loose in the wind. She was a blocky woman, of obvious Dutch ancestry, with thick shoulders and hands that were well used. She brought the snowmobile to a neat stop, right in front of Carpenter and clumped off of it in her hardy winter boots. Her eyes twinkled with amusement as she assessed her former husband standing in the middle of the road. Joanie knew his moods well. She never showed surprise, just an attitude of resigned acceptance. This attitude was often reflected in her posture; a turning in of the shoulders and slumping of head, mimicking submission. However, when she actually talked to him, her voice was strident and strong, her southwestern Texas drawl making her sound like she would be very at home on horseback or an oil rig. In reality, both were true; she'd grown up rough. Joanie had learned to make her way by using her considerable body strength, natural ability, and skillfulness with her hands. She was "no stinking violet", as she was fond of saying. She was a physical powerhouse, with strong legs, wide flat feet, and a broad jowly face. In spite of this sense of toughness emanating from her, Joanie's crowning glory – her lustrous hair, gave her a very feminine vulnerability and the sexual confidence of a late forties-something year old. She was all woman and a lot of it. That strength was what her ex always counted on to pull him out of his oft ill-fated jams. This morning, though, she had not come to deliver good news.

"You know, old man, you can run, and you can hide, but you can't get away from your own mistakes. Your karma will overtake you sooner or later. The Chiefs are launching an official investigation into your taking unauthorized leave of the fire staging area. You might have caught a break, though; they've asked Chief Hope to head it up."

Carpenter stomped at the snow on his boots and grumbled under his breath, "Some break, right at the balls."

"Oh, come on, you know she's going to be more considerate of you, if for no other reason than you're kind of related to me. Put that aside, she really does try to be fair."

"How much trouble am I in?" he asked.

"Fire Dog, you took a water tanker from an active wildland fire without permission. There was a dead firefighter along your route. What are you asking?" Joanie asked this with dispassionate exasperation.

"Well, I certainly don't know how the guy died," he replied defensively.

"The autopsy is still not back, but these are all the things that Chief Hope will have to look into and report back to the Chiefs Association Board. What I don't understand is why you did it. Why did you de-mob illegally? As long as you've been around fighting fires, it just doesn't make any sense. You know the protocol."

Carpenter stared at her for a long moment then he made a decision. "Come up to the barn, I've got something to show you."

Joanie pushed the snowmobile into the mouth of his driveway and trudged behind him up the icy slope of his drive and behind his A-frame cabin to the barn that she had helped him build. It was warmed inside by a small iron wood burner. He didn't keep animals since Joanie left. There was just some equipment and a couple old rockers placed near the stove. He kept a beat-up metal perker on it when it was chilly and automatically reached up on a small shelf, took down two cups and poured each of them a cup of "cowboy coffee".

"Now, Joanie, we've had our differences over all these years, but we've always trusted each other. If I tell you this, I have to swear you to secrecy. Can you agree?"

"What the hell? You got something to say man, just say it."

"No! This is more important than you can ever guess. I want your pledge and I want it now or you can just get back on your scooter and off my land."

"Okay, okay," Joanie said with some exasperation. "Fine, you have my promise. When have I ever let you down, huh? Name it."

"Listen, woman, I'm serious. Do I have your pledge?"
She nodded and mumbled an uh-huh, as she took a deep swig of coffee.

"Alright," he sighed and started moving stuff around in the barn. He then opened a trap door in the floor. "Come here."

"When did you put that in?" Joanie asked. She never heard an answer because she was aghast at what she saw. Inside the trap door, Carpenter was standing over a wooden crate of tiny gold nuggets.

Joanie shook her head in disbelief. Here we go she thought. Some men found trouble and headed the other way. Some didn't know they'd found it until it was upon them and then didn't recognize the situation until they were fighting for their lives, sanity, money, women or whatever the trouble brought. Carpenter was of the latter ilk.

Of course, once he was in the fight, his pride saw winning as his only objective. Looking at this chest of flaky gold, she knew Carpenter and trouble were about to go to the mat.

Chapter 2

Chiefs of the Trinity

Investigation

I snapped my fingers signaling the dog to heel. The large chocolate chessie came bounding out of the trees and into my path, grinning like a kid in a candy store.

"Don't you flush out any animal dens this morning?" I warned as I bent to give her a head rub and an affectionate pat on the rump. "That was the biggest skunk I have ever seen that chased you yesterday. I didn't know they even grew that large."

The dog cocked her head as if she understood language and playfully romped around my legs. Chuckling to myself, I thought she definitely understood "skunk", after an incident as a younger doggy, when she rooted out a nest and was thoroughly sprayed.

I had the unpleasant experience of giving her a tomato juice bath. I started a light jog, and the dog ran ahead of me. I turned off of the main drag, Trinity Pines Drive, one of only three paved roads in the community, onto steep graveled and dirt rutted, Pine Forest Road. The big dog stopped and looked at me in surprise because this wasn't the usual route, for Chez loved exploring this little hamlet as much as I did. Each house was different, custom designed by the owner, and in this mountainous setting situated at interesting elevations; some surrounded by trees, others pastureland, with streams intertwining throughout. Besides the Shasta-Trinity National Forest surrounded the community and at times jutted into it on what the residents called "The Boots". It was a nickname given as much to describe the shape of the areas as to poke fun at the animosity often felt by the local landowners toward the Forest Service for its sometimes-high-handed handling of communications in matters that affected this little burg. With 75% of the entire county being public lands, controlled by the state and federal government, most people in the area had some pretty strong opinions about the feds. Since moving to the area permanently, I have worked hard to put this place on the federal radar. It was the only way to get community assistance and funding.

"Let's get home, Chez. We have a house guest, you know," the dog acted very reluctant to change the routine. "Sorry, when Momma visits, it requires all hands-on-deck. I told Pete the same thing this morning before I left so that he could get up and get the coffee going. Since you can't do that, no grumbling from the peanut gallery."

We climbed the sharp hill on Pine Forest Road pass the 'Pee Paw Mountain' Donkey Ranch. The old half deaf man, Trader Jim, that lived there was out, as usual, shoveling feed and talking loud to his donkeys. He had about six of them right now.

They came and went as he sold or traded them off. Chez loved to bark at them and pretend that she was going to run into their pasture and chase them. This would set Trader Jim's aged miniature poodle off. The poor unclipped thing would just about break its neck trying to get off its leash thinking he needed to protect his territory. Why Trader Jim had a poodle in these rugged hills and on his rough shod place was beyond me. The guy was certainly a well-known eccentric. Everyone was surprised that the old timey mountain man treated me with such respect. It was because Trader Jim, who was the town's oldest living resident, knew something of my family's history in the area and he liked what I was trying to do for the place.

I threw up my hand and waved, yelling, "Hey Jim!"

He couldn't hear me, but I saw him wave back as I trotted a little on the downhill slope of the road. At the bottom of the hill, we turned left onto Bear Rock Road and slowed at the Grotto which was just on the back side of 'Pee Paw Mountain'. It was a cool shady glade of Incense Cedar trees, wood ferns and a year-round bubbling brook curving around the back side of the high hill of 'Pee Paw Mountain'.

It was one of our favorite places to stop for a quick rest and forest exploration before heading home. Although, I was in a hurry this morning, the place called to me. I stopped and sat on a large stump. I really needed a few moments of meditation. Chez looked at me expectantly, she was so tuned to my moods.

"Let's just take a few minutes to catch our breath. I know I said we needed to get back home. Just a quick Selah. Okay?"

The dog was happy to saunter off to splash in the stream, even though, it was ice cold from the unseasonable snow fall the night before. The Grotto was so canopied by cedars and other evergreens that it had no snow on the ground, just a little left in the trees that the warming morning sun had not melted away yet. Some of the fragrant drops fell lightly on me as I sat on a tree stump thinking of the problems I had to face today.

I had to launch an investigation into Carpenter's behavior. It was touchy with my Assistant Chief being his ex. The couple was still close in most ways of a long-term marriage. It was more like they just maintained separate houses. With the involvement of the dead or murdered fire fighter, I knew this might be out of my depth. Add that to my mother's visit for the first time since we'd moved to the mountains and my plate felt a little full. In most cases having "Alley Cat" around was a handful in and of itself.

Mentally using my mother's nickname, a family joke, I knew that I was irritated. I took a few deep breaths of the sweet clear air and remembered that I had promised Pete not to let mother's criticisms get to me. Pete, who had lost his mother recently, kept reminding me that I was lucky mine was alive, well enough to travel and enjoy life.

"Time to get moving, Chez," I called to the dog. We reluctantly left our little oasis and walked down the road toward the house.

The huge rock with cave openings called Bear Rock came into view. The road was named after the cave rock, where young bears sometimes still find their way to hibernate and wander around in spring. As I turned down the long driveway, the dog came bounding over the low rough hewn rock wall that bordered along the front of my property. The wall had been built by my great, great grandfather Skinner when he homesteaded the land in the 1800's. Everyone in the family was amazed that I was able to claim the property. It was still on the books. All I had done was prove my rights to it. That was more than thirty years ago and after paying some back taxes that had been quite low, I was able to title the property in my name. The odd thing was that my grandpapa had been paying the taxes until he passed away. No one in the family knew about it.

I had decided to do some research on the family history and happened upon the heir information. Grandpapa had just passed away a few months before that, so the county's small, undermanned tax department had not yet laid claim to the property.

I mused on this as I approached my house. It was a two-story cedar log cabin that Pete and I designed ourselves. We had it built by a local master craftsman. The house faced south on the highest point of the property with a view of Dubakella Mountain and "the boots". On the western side of the house was the national forest and on the north side was a brook that bubbled down to a stream at the bottom of the hill that the house sat on. The setting was ideal as far as I was concerned. We'd torn down the old one room shack that my great, great grandfather had built out of rough-hewn logs a few generations back. It had pretty much fallen down and looked like every kind of animal in the forest at one time or another had sought shelter in it.

Seeing my mother relaxing on the expansive deck with a mug of coffee, made me stop in wonderment at the twists and turns that life sometimes takes. Here we were in one of the most pristine places on earth and it was a place that God had prepared for us long before even my mother was born. I was really hit with the Bible scripture: I go to prepare a place for you, for in my Father's house there are many mansions. [1]

I went into the storage house and set out a bowl of food for Chez. Her water bucket was full, and she had drunk plenty at the Grotto. I headed inside, grabbed a cup of delicious smelling Kona coffee, and sat down on the deck next to my mother with a deep sigh of well being.

"I can't believe how quiet and peaceful it is here," my mother said. Just as I was going to nod in agreement, she broke the spell of contentment.

"It is such a contrast to that time I had to come out to Hawaii to see about you."

As only my mother could do, this sent me immediately into reliving a high stress time in my life. My mother has the knack of showing up to "see about" me when I happen to be going through some major problem in my life. It was uncany since we often lived thousands of miles apart even when I was a child. When questioned why she'd chosen that particular time to pay a visit, she'd always say, "You have to watch as well as pray."

As my mother had probably intended, her comment took me back to another beautiful place, one that was not so peaceful for me, though it had produced great grace and growth in my life; Hawaii, over thirty years ago. It didn't even feel like that was me.

Chapter 3

A Mighty Long Way

Holoholo

Hope sprung from the bed and bolted out the back door. She was halfway across the lush expansive lawn, almost to the white sandy beach shore and soothing, gentle waves before she fell on her face. As the turmoil in her stomach turned into dry heaves, she wondered, where were the folks that were supposed to love her. Where was Faith when she really needed her? Don't be stupid, she chided herself, Faith was where you left her, 6000 miles away. The thought of her sister, her family being so far away brought loud uncontrollable sobs out of her depths. She lay in the grass and gave into her grief and despair with sweet abandon. How could this be happening? This could not be her fate, she almost prayed, but she knew it was her path. She could feel it settling on her shoulders like a woolen shawl or mantel, weighing her to Mother Earth, sloping her posture to fit the vision and heaviness of responsibility, even expectation of the collective sub- consciousness of previous incarnations of Self. That Self now screamed for her mother or sister or aunt or some familiar.

Go ahead, do it the way you know how to do. Surely you can improve this "time". Reminder that it is "just" eyesight, temperament, timing, faith, hope and a whole combination of things that none of us really understand. We have only discerned darkly. Remember that you're a soul path traveler. Surely, she was losing her mind or having a "nervous breakdown", as Doc had suggested. Indeed, she was paralyzed with worry. She knew he was manipulative and couldn't be trusted, but rationality now escaped her. Maybe Doc was right, she was having a nervous breakdown. Who wouldn't with all the illusions she'd been fed and the reality distortions, ever since the trip to the Volcano, her whole life had changed.

Her friends' car had suddenly stopped in the middle of road, halfway up the deserted road to the Kilauea Volcano. The volcano was erupting so there was little or no visibility because of the 'vog'. The eruption had been going on for months so the vog was really thick. She had learned that vog is a hazy mixture which the volcano spewed of SO2 gas and aerosols (tiny particles or droplets) which are primarily sulfuric acid and other sulfate compounds. They thought the vog may have caused the problems with the old hippy jalopy that her travelling companions, Godwin and Deana had bought from their friends, Ted, and Viv.

Deana was a dancer and Hope's friend from San Francisco where they had been sharing a lovely Victorian with two other close friends. Deana had met Godwin on her last trip to Hawaii and they'd fallen in love. Deana was a true love child with flowers in her hair all the time and sometimes she walked around nude from waist up. She was a beautiful young woman with soft blond hair halfway down her back, when dressed, she wore flowing skirts and capes. She oozed peaceful warmth and had a Mona Lisa smile like she's about to impart some special wisdom just for you that would change your life. She came back to the 'mainland' to handle some business before returning to be with Godwin. It took longer than Deana thought so she'd moved in with Hope and friends until she settled a sad messy divorce that involved property.

Deana invited Hope to come to Hawaii with her when she returned for a visit. Deana kept saying that she knew Hope would love the place. Hope was persuaded to go, even though, she was living a very busy city life, and the decision gave her some trepidation. Hope had a small fledging wholesale specialty bakery, supplying health food stores and cafeterias. However, the young couple that she employed promised to keep the business running while she was on her 'holoholo', as Deana said it was called in Hawaiian.

Her guy, Godwin, a handsome high energy man, was working as a sailing ship restoration specialist and boat builder. He was also a sailor and world traveler. He was best known for his prolific artistic ability to make large intricate sculptures and paint abstract complicated canvasses. He'd painted a Sanskrit symbol on the rear of the jalopy.

Just as they were pushing the car to the side of the road, a big new sedan came floating out of the thickening vog and slowed as it approached the three stranded travelers. The car was occupied by an older white couple. They stopped, but didn't let their window down, instead they just starred at Hope like they had never seen a black person. Hope felt self conscious, although she knew she looked 'presentable'. She'd worn her gold and brown paisley antique dress with long flute sleeves, pulled her afro into a large top poof accented with handcrafted earrings and a beautiful pair of clogs from a shop in the city.

Finally, they let the window down, then the woman pointed to the back of the broken-down car, which had the Sanskrit symbol painted on it, looked directly at Hope and said,

"We only stopped because we saw your aura then we saw the symbol on the car. Are you on a destiny quest? Well, it looks like you are, even if you don't know it. We can take you as far as the Volcano House. Unless you have a room reservation there already, probably won't be anything available. They are always booked solid."

Godwin thanked them and the three piled into the back seat and introduced themselves. The woman turned all the way around and starred at Hope for a long moment.

She said, "This is a very significant journey for you. It will affect your destiny path for the rest of your life. A strange yang energy happens when the volcano erupts. I'm a Spiritualist and Empath so I see how it affects people. My husband here is a non-believer."

"Stop right there," her husband interrupted. "I'm a geophysicist – retired. I seek reasons and provable truths. Volcanoes are usually found near the borders of tectonic plates that are violently either pushing or pulling at each other.

Mysteriously, however, volcanoes sometimes erupt in the middle of these plates instead. The culprits behind these outbursts might be giant pillars of hot molten rock known as mantle plumes, jets of magma rising up from near the Earth's core to penetrate overlying material like a blow torch. Still, decades after mantle plumes were first proposed, controversy remains as to whether or not they exist. The concept of mantle plumes began with the enigma of the Hawaiian volcanoes, which dwell more than 2,000 miles from the nearest plate boundary. Scientists think that as the Pacific plate slid over a "hot spot" a line of volcanoes blossomed. These are provable facts. My wife only has her theories."

His wife folded her arms, "Have most of my predictions come true or not?"

The man hesitated then said, "Yes, dear. You've called it right a time or two."

Chapter 4

Chiefs of the Trinity

Blood

My mother was rambling. I had to renew my focus because her remarks had sent me off on a mental tangent. She was bragging about her recent trip to Chicago where she visited her best friend who was now married to her ex-husband. She was so proud of the fact that they all still got along. I marveled at her "family is family" attitude. This conversation brought me smack dab back to my immediate dilemma, what to do about Carpenter and by association, Joanie. Because indeed, Joanie had a lot of my mother's attitude in her relationship with Carpenter. They were divorced, but still very involved in each other's lives.

I once asked Joanie why she dealt with Carpenter and she said, "I just love his mind." A far cry from my stance of when I'm done, I'm done; right, wrong, or indifferent; just ask my first husband, Doc.

Chez came around from the back yard and stretched out on the deck near Mama. It amazed me that Mama liked animals because she seldom found people that she took to easily. She reached over and stroked Chez's coat and they seemed very comfortable with each other. The mountain morning sun, bubbling brook and swaying scented Sugar Pines lulled us into a relaxed state.

But the thought of Mama and Joanie's attitudes gave me an idea of a possible approach to the Carpenter investigation. It may not be a miracle, but it would be a tale of miracles, a way to spin flax into gold, so to speak. Little did I know how literal those peaceful morning musings would become.

Pete was out in the powerhouse, giving Mama a lesson on our solar power generation system. He was proud of the off-grid system that he'd designed with my help.

Sitting at my eagle's nest desk on the second floor, overlooking the panoramic view across my land all the way to Dubakella Mountain, I reached for the phone and dialed Joanie's number. This time of morning, she was often in her greenhouse or out in her gardens, depending on the weather, which meant that I would have to let the phone ring for a long time because she didn't use an answering machine. However, this morning, she did not answer at all, so I tried her on her fireman's handheld communication device, which she always had with her; using her call numbers, I asked her to contact me by landline. A few minutes later my phone rang. It was showing Carpenter's ID.

"Hello, hey Joanie, is everything alright? You at the ex's house?"

"No, everything is not alright. We need to talk."

"Yes, okay, that's why I'm calling. Can I stop by your place in a few?"

"No, come by Carpenter's. He needs to show you something."

Uh oh, I'm thinking this could be "something" serious. Joanie didn't have that humor in her voice that she usually carried like she was just about to tell a funny joke. I suddenly felt too tired to get up but knew I couldn't rest. This feeling was always a sign that something complicated was headed my way. I asked Pete to take Momma into town to pick up a couple of items for a dish she wanted to prepare while I went over to Carpenter's to meet Joanie.

Pete said, "I hope she finds what she wants. You know Hayfork is not exactly the soul food capitol of the world."

Hayfork was 20 miles away and the nearest town of any size; a place where the women were beautiful and smart with stupid names. There was Booger, a tall naturally gorgeous girl with blond wavy hair down to her bottom; Casey, a petite athlete with shiny thick long dark hair that showed her native heritage; Crystal, with flaming red thick tangled hair and ethereal clear skin whose clothes made her look like a princess in a fantasy tale (in fact, she was an author of fantasy books); Ginger, a raven haired, lavender eyed Elizabeth Taylor in National Velvet lookalike, whose last name really was Snapp; Buffalo Woman, a stately business owner who dressed like a squaw and whose face stubbornly held the bloodline of some determined native ancestor even with the European infusions; and Molly, who was so warm, friendly and lovely, that when she smiled (and she smiled often), you just wanted to say, "Good Golly, Miss Molly!"

The men were mostly not attractive; dirty from some kind of rough work or other, drank and smoked too much, carried guns around, would cheat on their woman if given a chance; somehow, you knew, when the chips were down, they could be counted on to get you out of just about any kind of a jam. Plus, they could repair or re-purpose most anything. Many of them were poets and musicians at heart.

The town was almost a movie version of genteel women and Wild West men. I really love the folks in that town even though Pete and I are the only black woman and black man living in the county permanently. I feel strong ties to the place. Of course, some of it has to do with my great, great grandfather having set up his camp, and trudged around the area a long time ago. It felt like home. Sometimes I could swear I can feel his spirit looking over my shoulder. I believe that Ancestral Memory is deeper than just the telling of family stories and history.

My great-great grandfather died long before I was born. His wife, my great-great grandmother lived until she was 111 years old and loved to sit on her porch at her farm and talk to my grandfather about family history. I was about 5 or 6 years old when she died. I used to tag along with my "Papa" when he'd go out to visit her. Grandma Skinner would say she didn't know why the Lord kept her here so long. Because I knew it always made her chuckle until her shoulders shook up and down relishing my role as the only great-great grandchild, I often liked to pipe up in my child's voice and say, "So you can talk to me, GG!"

All of these random thoughts and remembrance of family were wandering through my head as I drove the little red Fire Chief's truck onto Carpenter's road.

His driveway was blocked with the Fire Department's snow mobile that mostly Joanie used because I couldn't handle the big awkward contraption.

As I walked up Carpenter's driveway, I had an inexplicable feeling that I was stepping back in time or history. It was not a comfortable experience. I kept walking towards his house. It was a feeling that I had once before of approaching predestination and looking through a glass darkly at a certain preordained fate or karma. I shook my head slightly to shake the feeling. It trailed behind me like volcano fog - vog.

"Good morning!" I shouted out so they'd know I was here.

Joanie came around the side of the house and said, "We're in the barn!"

I walked into the rough-hewn structure with a small stove going inside for warmth and Carpenter stood up with his back to me and asked if I wanted coffee. I said yes, out of courtesy because I really didn't like "cowboy coffee" – too strong for me. He handed me a small hot cup, but still hadn't looked at me. My intuition was firing on all cylinders.

"Thanks, okay guys, what's happening?" I said sitting gingerly in a small armless old rocking chair close to the heating source.

Carpenter finally turned and looked at me. He looked haunted and scared. He started to speak then cleared his throat when nothing came out. Joanie was standing near some things piled in a corner of the barn watching him intently.

"Best I show you and get it over with – see for yourself," Carpenter said as he went towards Joanie, then reached down and opened up the floor. I got up and eased toward the hole, hoping it wasn't a big snake or something else crazy. It was glittery!

"What is this?! It looks like gold sand with nuggets! What am I seeing here?"

I looked at them dumbfounded.

"This is why Carpenter left the staging area so unceremoniously," Joanie said.

"Okay, sit back down and I will tell you what happened," Carpenter said.

"No, this has to be done formally. I can't just do this haphazardly. This is some serious shit!" I said with a growing sense of alarm. This looked like a major theft and there was this matter of the dead fire fighter.

"Let's go to the Fire Hall, sit down in the conference room and record this. I don't know the whole story here, but I know it could go legal real fast so let me be clear, I'm now acting in my appointed capacity as the Investigator in your case. So, we do it by the book, Carpenter, to protect both of us. Understood?" I said firmly using my best authoritative Chief's voice. Considering who I was dealing with, I was slightly surprised when he readily agreed.

The snow on the main paved roads had melted by now so Joanie and Carpenter got in his truck, and I eased mine out of his driveway and waited until they pulled in front of me so that I was behind them all the way to the Fire Hall. I couldn't help thinking about all that gold in his makeshift floor safe. Where the hell did it come from?

Since we were a Volunteer Fire Department, the building was not manned unless we were staging for a fire or having a community meeting. Joanie was already out of the truck and unlocking the building when I parked so the lights and heat were on in the conference room by the time I'd gathered myself and entered the room. Carpenter was pacing. Joanie was sitting serenely. She was always especially cool during a crisis.

I had attended a few incidents with her before, like; house fires, car accidents, suicides, evacuations and an even an avalanche. I could count on Joanie to be calm and efficient. I took out my keys and unlocked the corner cabinet where we kept the tape recorder for recording community meetings. I set it up with a pad and the file.

I listened incredulously to his story. It still didn't reveal the source of the gold.

"I'm going to review your statement. You saw the guy on the road and stopped to see about him. You saw he was dead. He was clutching these old saddle bags for dear life. You didn't recognize him, nor had you seen him before. The gold was too tempting. You took it, got scared, left the fire staging area and high-tailed it home. You have no idea the source of this gold. You dug a hole under your barn and hid it there anyway. Where are these old saddle bags, still in your barn?"

I stated in as neutral a voice as I could muster. Carpenter nodded his head yes.

I sat back in my chair, closed my eyes and my memory kicked in. In my family, everyone is always surprised at how I can remember details of things that happened when I was young. This triggered a story that my great-great grandmother told me and my Papa (her oldest grandson) once or twice about her husband, my great-great grandfather, John "Mule" Skinner.

She had harrumphed, "That dang Mule left bags of gold up in those mountains. He 'llowed he didn't want none of that blood money!"

My eyes popped open, and I was off my GGs porch and back in the conference room. I opened the file that had been given to me on the case and read some of the entries. Indeed, the body had been located on the edge of the fire area just where I surmised, near the Natural Bridge. The autopsy, nor the identity, had come in yet.

Jesse Whyte was head of the County Fire Chief's Association. He'd appointed me to investigate this incident since it involved someone from my crew, also I felt that he trusted me. No one could have ever guessed that the two of us would form a bond. He was a rugged, handsome sixty-year-old woodsman with a shock of snowwhite hair, who had been raised in these mountains and I am a black woman with newcomer ideas. For a number of reasons, though, we worked well together and developed a great professional relationship. Like me, Head Chief Whyte was a conservationist who believed in land stewardship and preventive fire management, especially in Rural Urban Interface areas, what is now being called RUIs, for short.

When I first became the Fire Chief for my township, he made it his business to set up a meeting with me. After a relatively brief conversation about a project that he wanted to implement at all of the County Fire Departments, I agreed to help get it off the ground; because it sounded awesome in terms of how it could help protect our communities and homes from wildfire. It also fit my idea of stewardship and community service. A life philosophy that over the years, I had developed not only a passion for, but felt it was the only enlightened way to live in society and on this earth.

With these thoughts on my heart, I bumped down the dirt roads in my little red truck from Carpenter's house to my own. We'd gone back over to his place so I could take photos of the "evidence" including the old, corroded leather saddle bags. Carpenter wasn't going anywhere, and Joanie said she would stay with him, in her capacity as the Deputy Chief. I had to give this situation some strategic thought.

Momma had the place lit up with something smelling good when I walked in, and I decided that I could think better with a good meal in my stomach. Chez was walking around the house in circles hoping for something to drop on the floor. She ignored me when I walked in and was trying to stay as close to Momma as her hard-earned indoor manners would allow.

"It smells good in here. When can we eat?" I asked as I lured Chez out the door with a dog biscuit which she left on the porch with a hurt look on her face as I closed the sliding glass door. Chez resignedly sat on her haunches and starred into the kitchen while I set the table. Momma had mercy on her and gave her a small piece of meat with a bone attached on a napkin. This seemed to satisfy her, and she got up on the seating bench that surrounded the porch and took her position as watch dog looking over the yard and down towards the stream at the bottom of the hill. This was one of her favorite spots to relax.

We ate the delicious meal in quiet contentment. My mother was an excellent cook. However, she was never generous about sharing her recipes or the kitchen. Therefore, I definitely did not measure up to her skill level and after Pete sang her praises for ten minutes, I made the excuse that I had to make an important call and went upstairs to my office. I sat there at my desk for a while, listening to Pete and Momma laughing and talking. They really got along well, as long as Pete lavished her with positive attention.

Momma liked to have her ego fed by men and Pete could be very charming most of the time. Momma never got along with my first husband, 'Doc', but Pete was known around town as a great diplomat. It was probably because of his upbringing as the son of a pastor and then his career after college as one of the first black IBM executives. In both roles, you have to be a people pleaser. He was also just a really nice guy who genuinely liked folks. He always says, just let him play golf or go fishing on his bass boat and he was "good". He was excellent at both. He loves living in this place of the wonderful, clear mountain lakes which were under-utilized because of distance from the cities, making the fish plentiful with firm meat from the cold pure waters. Pete often goes over to the various lakes and brings home rainbow trout, bass, crappy, bluegill, and one of my favorites, kokanee, which is basically a freshwater salmon. Pete is great about cleaning the fish and breaking out his grill on the shady side of the house for an impromptu fish fry. All I have to do for the meal is a make a salad and sometimes hush puppies.

My mind tends to meander around when I have a thorny problem to work through and this helped me realize that I needed more information before I could proceed any further. I picked up the phone and dialed the Head Chief's number.

He had caller ID so when he answered, he just started talking, "I was planning to call you this evening, but since you've called me, hold on and let me get to my desk. I have news that you will want to know on the case."

I still hadn't said a word. I listened to his footsteps as he walked quickly to his office. My anxiety rose up again and the big meal was forming a knot in my stomach.

"Okay, the identification and the cause of death are in. The guy died of a heart attack. He wasn't even supposed to be on the Incident. He was a recent volunteer and not even certified yet. According to his resume, he'd had training years ago when he was much younger and used to live here. He had not completed his equipment certification. He'd listed his next of kin as a sister who lives in Hawaii with her family. She has been notified and is on her way here to claim the body. She told me that she tried to talk him out of moving back here and was really alarmed when he told her he had joined the Fire Department. Evidently, he lied on his application about his physical condition. He didn't say that he had a heart stent! Well, the over exertion caused his death. What I can't make out is how he got any assignment at all and also where his body was found. The only crews that we had assigned over there for that area were the water tankers for filling up at ponds near the Natural Bridge. This guy's name was Dwayne Dixon. When his sister gets here, I'll find out more about him. I hadn't had any dealings with the fellow because he hadn't taken my certification classes yet. Did you know him?"

"No, Head Chief, I don't think so. I may have some answers for you on what the late Mr. Dixon was up to. When can you come out here to Dubakella Mountain? There is something related to all of this that I need to show you. It may offer some clues as why this guy was in the wrong place at the wrong time. Also, I have taken a written, sworn and witnessed statement from Carpenter as to why he de-mobilized illegally. It might be good if you can come before Mr. Dixon's sister gets here. This information is probably pertinent to any discussion that you have with the Dixon family."

"Okay, let me look at my schedule and I'll get back with you pronto," Head Chief Whyte said and rang off abruptly, as was his manner. From his side of the county, it was at least an hour and a half each way to our side of the mountain. It was really a day trip for Head Chief Whyte. I hoped he could make it here soon.

I walked slowly back downstairs. Pete and Momma were sitting on the deck with Chez. Pete still smoked and though Momma had given it up, it didn't seem to bother her that Pete was enjoying his customary cigarillo. All three looked around expectantly at me when I opened the screen slider. I knew they wanted to know what I was running around all day doing so I pulled up a deck chair and plopped down with a sigh.

"Momma, do you remember any of the stories that GG Skinner used to tell about this place?" Pete put his cigarillo in the ash tray, got up and went into the kitchen.

"Well, Daddy used to go out to her farm a lot and sit around either on the porch or by the kitchen stove running his mouth with her. I was the youngest and my mother was sick. She wanted me near her all the time. When she died, I was only 5 years old and then I went to live with Aunt Lee in the city after that. I have very little memory of her. When you were a real little girl, Daddy liked to show off his only grandchild and took you around to GG Skinner's a lot since she was blessed with a really long life."

Pete came back and handed me a glass of my favorite pinot noir from one of several local wineries in the area. He looked concerned, "What's going on, Hope?"

I took a deep breath and said, "You won't believe this. It seems that Carpenter has come into the possession of, literally, a pot of gold. Before you ask too many questions, remember that this is an official investigation. Fortunately, I just found out that the fire fighter that died at the scene was not murdered. Here is where it gets tricky, though. Carpenter found the body. Instead of calling it in, he stole these old saddle bags that were full of gold from the dead guy and fled the scene without letting anyone know what was happening."

Pete had a "mind like a steel trap" and he seemed to grasp the scene and situation immediately, "You're asking about your ancestral stories. Is this related to the one about your great-great grandfather being involved with helping some kid who survived the massacre at the Natural Bridge way back then? The lost gold stories were true?!"

"That's what I think, after looking at the evidence and taking his statement. I mean this is pretty crazy. Here's another rub, the dead guy's last name is Dixon. My research of those days showed that there was a Sheriff Dixon involved in that horrible massacre and debacle. Head Chief says that the guy recently moved to the area but had spent time here as a kid. My imagination is running away with me. Could it be that, after generations, this whole mess is going to be ginned back up."

We sat in stunned silence, contemplating the karmic arc. It felt almost surreal.

"You all need legal advice. You are talking about a fortune. This could get litigious real fast. Whose gold is it after all this time and the macabre, bizarre circumstances around finding this lost treasure?" Pete asked in a contemplatively way.

"You're right. I'm going to call Graham in the morning," I said and relaxed for the first time all afternoon. We sat on the deck in contented silence; I sipped my favorite wine and watched a beautiful mountain sunset that turned the whole sky a fiery then soft red. We did not go inside until the little Spotted Owls started their hooting. They were an endangered species, but we had a lot of them here, thanks to the many conservationists and environmentalists who lived in these mountains and fought to preserve their habitats.

Chapter 5

Chiefs of the Trinity

Legalese

Graham Michaels was an attorney and neighbor who had lived in this little isolated community for years. He'd been a high-powered L.A. corporate litigator who burned out during a nasty divorce. Apparently, he gave her everything except his mountain home which she didn't want anyway, and he dropped out up here. He ran a small practice from home of mostly real estate and occasionally criminal law.

I didn't even take my usual morning walk with Chez before I called him. He was always cordial to me since I had bought several lots adjacent to my place and he'd handled the legal paperwork for me. When I told him that I had some important Fire Department business that we needed his counsel on, he said if I gave him coffee, he'd meet me at the Fire Hall in an hour. I could walk up to the Fire Hall in ½ hour, so I agreed. This way I could kill two birds with one stone; get in a walk with the dog and handle some of this business.

Before I could get out the door, the phone on my desk rang. It was Head Chief Whyte who let me know that he would drive out to our side of the mountain in the morning. I thanked him, slipped into my hiking boots, grabbed the leash just in case Chez was feeling too frisky for me to be able to have a quiet meeting with the attorney. She usually knew she'd better behave herself when she saw me with a leash, or she would get tied up. Sometimes she got kind of hyped up as most Retrievers do. However, by the time we arrived at the Fire Hall, which is situated at the top of a good size hill, Chez was ready to stretch out in the sun. As soon as I got one of the big bay doors pulled open, she found her a spot where the sun could warm her fur and laid on her side with her eyes closed. When Graham arrived, she lifted her head just enough to make sure she recognized the person, thumped her tail on the concrete a couple times and went right back to her nap.

In the conference room, I went through the details of the case with Graham, he sat looking as stunned at the events as I was when I first realized what this could be. He reviewed his notes, asked a few clarifying questions on Carpenter's statement, then sat back quietly in the chair thinking it over. He wrote a note then looked at me somberly.

"I'm going to write up an affidavit on this in the next couple of hours and I want you and Carpenter to sign it. Additionally, I'm going to write my recommendations on how this "treasure" should be handled and possibly disbursed. I'd like to get the documents approved and signed this afternoon before you meet with Head Chief Whyte tomorrow. By the way, do you want me in the meeting with Head Chief, as legal counsel for the department?" he asked. (He handled our occasional legal matters for a small fee.)

"Let me think about that and get back to you this afternoon when we meet on the affidavit. I'm not sure how much finessing this is going to need politically. If you're going to be around tomorrow, I'd definitely like you on standby. I think that would make me feel better or at least more prepared for any curve balls that Head Chief Whyte might have for us."

I called over to Carpenter's and told them about the legal document meeting with Graham and the meeting with Head Chief. He and Joanie said they were on board, so I went about the rest of my day with some sense of peace. My mother and Pete agreed that I had dotted the I's and crossed the T's as far as I could without anyone landing in jail. Carpenter could possibly be charged with theft. The attorney thought that was a distance possibility because he had a plan to avert it. He would present it to us this afternoon when we all trudged back to the Fire Hall.

Attorney Michaels' plan was brilliant, even Carpenter agreed on that. I just had to sell it to the Head Chief. Some nuances to Carpenter's story we had to finesse to make it work. It was not lying just 'adjusting' it so it would be fair to all involved. Surely Head Chief will go for it because it was a sensible way to handle a once in a century situation, so to speak, or as Graham said, a "100- year flood phenomena".

Head Chief arrived at the appointed time the next morning. I'd made him my favorite; Kona coffee and my mother had baked a coffee cake. She excelled at baking, so we sipped the aromatic hot liquid and savored the rich pastry before we got down to business. Jesse Whyte had a soulful Sam Elliot look and demeanor, like he knew it was going to be some BS, but he'd hear you out before he killed you.

"Head Chief, this is going to be hard for you to believe," I started cautiously.

"Try me! I've been up in these hills for a minute so not much surprises me!"

"Well, you know I came here because my great-great grandfather had this land that my family and I managed to hang onto for several generations. Pete and I love this area of California, so we decided to homestead the place and built our log house here. What you may not know is that my great-great grandfather played a small role in the Natural Bridge saga. He helped one of the survivors who was a direct descendant of Chief Pentallis. This descendant offered him the location of a gold treasure, which he turned down on principle because he saw it as blood money. Well, it looks like this man Dixon found it! As the tale goes, at the time of the massacre, there was a Sheriff Dixon in charge, and they say he conducted the raid on the sacred grounds. The missing saddlebags with the gold treasure were never found.

Carpenter came across Dixon's body when going to fill his water tanker. He stopped to see if he could help the guy and near his body, he stumbled on the old saddlebags. He picked them up and realized they were unusual in age and weight, so he looked inside. What he saw scared the "b'jesus" out of him and thrilled his working man's heart, all at the same time. Seriously, who wouldn't be knocked off their game if they found a cache of gold laid out on the ground, next to a dead body? Carpenter is an honest, hard-working guy. His wife of many years broke it off with him when she got promoted at the fire department and he didn't. It's been a rough stretch for him so let's try to be understanding here of the poor decision making on his part.

However, our department's legal counsel has a proposal to fairly dispense with the found treasure. He's written it up and I would like you to read it and see if you think it works for the community and all concerned," I handed Chief Whyte the bulleted proposal. He began to read and then looked at me with a dawning realization.

"Yes, it could solve a few issues and help us meet some major goals," I said.

"1. The gold is considered recovered treasure, so Carpenter gets a finder's fee.

2. The Fire Chiefs Association gets all the gold and dispenses it as grants to the other Fire Departments that have their books in order. That accomplishes two goals that you have been pushing: a. they get their financial houses in order and b. they get money to upgrade equipment, facilities, etc. which has an immediate benefit to their local areas.

3. The Big Red Truck educational and fire prevention program that you have been working so hard to get off the ground gets funding because the Fire Chiefs Association can resource it with this recovered treasure.

It's a win-win for the entire County!" I finished excitedly as I thought about the possibilities of preventing house, forest, and wild land fires. The Big Red Truck was Head Chief Whyte's brainchild and I thought this would be the closer for his decision.

"Wow! This is a lot. Let's go have a look, talk to Carpenter and it gives me a minute to see the cons because I definitely see the pros," Head Chief stood up. He was a man of action. I knew that he just needed to move around so he could think.

"I'll drive," I said, turned out the lights and we headed for my little red truck. Head Chief was silent all the way to Carpenter's. When we turned in the driveway, I saw Joanie and Graham's vehicles, so I knew Carpenter suspected we were coming. They were waiting in the barn with large mugs of coffee which Head Chief and I turned down when offered. They had the saddlebags and gold displayed on a table. Head Chief knew everyone, so he just launched right into his questions, which Graham answered for us and Carpenter. I could see him coming around to our way of thinking. He had one last concern that he voiced and I think all of us had it tickling the backs of our mines.

"What about the Wintu? Do you think they will want to lay claim to this gold?" Head Chief Whyte asked.

Graham gave his opinion, which was that they would benefit as well, since they had a fire department on their reservation and many of them lived in other burgs in the county that would benefit from the grants. Graham contended that the Dixon family was not entitled to any compensation since it was technically never their treasure, and the guy was trying to steal it when he died. However, to keep the matter in hand, he suggested that the Fire Chiefs Association offer to give him a fireman's funeral and pay for it. A fireman's funeral was a very high honorable send off and his reputation would be intact. He really should not have been there and was at the fire scene illegally. Chief Whyte wanted Graham to make a presentation to the Executive Committee of the Association and I suggested that the Association pay Graham a fee out of the proceeds as well and have him handle all of the necessary transactions and paperwork. Graham took possession of the already inventoried gold. He and Head Chief would take it to a safe deposit box for now until a broker was contacted. It was going to be in the millions of dollars when the exchange was made. I was going to finish my report and have Graham review it before it was published to the Association.

"Okay, if all hearts and minds are clear, we will proceed with the plan," I stated to vigorous nods all around, especially Carpenter, who looked relieved, like a big burden had been lifted off his wry shoulders.

Over the next few days, we carried out the plan, which was accepted in an emergency meeting of the Fire Chiefs Exec. Board. The Dixon man's sister, Camilla Tyner (married name), attended part of the meeting and was more than happy to let the Association put on the funeral. She'd come all the way from Hawaii and had no idea what her brother's life was like here or how to set up anything for a funeral.

Strangely enough, when I met her, we realized that we knew each other from years ago, during my time of living in the Hawaiian Islands when I was married to Doc, my first husband. She'd been a "Beach Mum" buddy. There'd been a group of young moms who brought our toddlers and pre-school age children for an almost daily romp on the beach near Puako. It was a small, loosely formed, community support group. We'd take turns watching over the kids, giving out drinks and snacks. Mostly we laid on our little, remote "neighborhood" beach, enjoying the sun and a little leisurely gossip.

There were four or five of us moms and the friendships were transient, not the kind you hold onto for a lifetime, but it was interesting to talk with her again. I had no idea about her background because when I knew Camilla, most of our conversations were about our children, husbands, and the family life that we were experiencing.

I remember that once when we were on the beach chatting, we realized that we'd been living in New York City's Greenwich Village at the same time, and had dated the same guy, who'd dumped us both and took off to Mexico to find himself. We'd both left New York and moved to California. She'd gone to Los Angeles for school, and I'd moved to San Francisco for business, before we ended up on the same beach at the same time on Hawaii's Big Island. Camilla had married into a well off, kama'aina, family of medical professionals and I had married Doc, who was working for the County Health Department as its Assistant Director.

We then moved out of the country for a couple years when Doc got an overseas appointment with the World Health Organization and that was the last time I'd seen or heard of Camilla. Now, here we were crisscrossing paths again in a complicated way; not that my situation in Hawaii wasn't complicated. As I drove slowly back across the mountain, I was thrown many, many years back, thinking of those Hawaiian times.

Chapter 6

A Mighty Long Way

Vog

Arriving at the Volcano House, they disembarked like grateful survivors of a shipwreck. Before Hope could make her exit, "Empath", as her husband called her, grabbed Hope's hand tightly and looked deeply into her eyes, then she gave her what, years later, Hope remembered as 'The Help' speech because she said the equivalent of the 'You is pretty. You is smart. You is kind,'; which is from a movie that came out years later and for some reason Hope always associated with what Empath intently messaged, "You're a beautiful, intelligent, good person. Do not allow anyone to destroy the Divine Gift of a wonderful spirit. Oh, and watch out for Pele. She's a jealous bitch!"

Then they were disappearing into the vog which seemed to obscure the sound of their car's motor, so it was eerily as if they were rising into the heavens. Hope stood in front of the hotel for a moment stunned into immobility by the woman's pronouncements and the sense of otherworldliness of the place. Then she walked slowly toward the lobby where she heard Godwin talking in an animated tone on the lobby phone. She noticed Deana at the hotel bar. Evidently, she had found someone who knew her. Deana was well known as a talented dancer. In Hawaii, great dancers, singers, musicians, and artists are revered. She was laughing and talking with the bartender and waitress.

There was only one table occupied in the lounge, so Hope went and sat at a corner table. She was deep in contemplation on the experiences she'd had so far on this holoholo trek and there was a lot to think about. Her revelry was interrupted when she heard her name. She looked around, astonished that the waitress was at the table and knew her by name.

"I was in Kona the other night and saw you sing at Akamai Barnes with Ted's band. You were great. Can I get you something to drink?" the kind eyed waitress asked.

Akamai Barnes was a tiki bar in Kona owned by a famous actor. It was the spot!

Hope had asked Ted if she could sit in for a song or two, when she and Deana had stopped by their house to see Viv, while the band was rehearsing. Hope sat in on the rehearsal and sang along on a couple songs. After the rehearsal, Ted told her he wanted her to sing a couple of the blues songs they had just done, at the tiki bar where they played. Hope was thrilled and honored. Ted used to play for some big names, like Diana Washington, before he landed on the beach in Kona. The thing that Hope really loved about Hawaii was that there was music everywhere. It seemed to infuse the life of the land, everyone in it and to float on the air like the scent of the plumeria bloom.

"Thanks, Ted and his band can make anybody sound good, even us amateurs," Hope said shyly to the young woman as she saw Godwin come into the room, walk up behind Deana, kiss her cheek, sit down at the bar, and start speaking urgently to her. He took his sketch pad out of his satchel, started drawing furiously as Deana spoke back to him. He listened intently for a while.

When the waitress brought Hope's drink, she said, "Looks like you all are stranded on the mountain. We're trying to see if we can get you some help with the car or a room, if we have any no shows which are rare here."

The room slowly filled with people. Hope relaxed, ate some "pupus" and enjoyed the ambience. Godwin and Deana were in conversations with folks at the bar; seemed to be enjoying themselves and not concerned about the car or the situation. The music was simple, really good Hawaiian slack key. Deana, who had studied dance at San Francisco State, could do almost any form, got up and did a graceful lovely traditional Hawaiian hula, to resounding applause. Godwin was sketching caricatures of various folks at the bar to everyone's amusement and delight. Hope admired the way they both lived their art. She was not as outgoing or sure of herself as they were, so she just enjoyed basking in the loving light her friends gave off. While she was a third wheel on this trip, for some reason, they were always inviting her and treated her like family.

Deana was always a kind person anyway and Godwin was just a great character who you couldn't help but love because he wrapped his arms, euphemistically, around anyone in his presence, like a force of kindness. Hope was really starting to enjoy this whole thing, in spite of the strange encounter with 'Empath' that had kind of given her a sense of foreboding. The atmosphere here was the very opposite of threatening. It was loving and it felt so natural. Hope hummed quietly to the music and sipped her drink. She was so relaxed and in her own space that she barely noticed the room was slowly emptying out and it was getting dark. Hope started to be concerned about their lodging for the night, so she walked over to the bar and asked Deana what they were going to do.

Before Deana answered, she felt almost a cold breeze as a couple of guys walked in and greeted the bartender and waitress loudly. One of them spoke to Godwin, Deana, and Hope by name. Hope did not recognize him. He was a handsome guy about her age with thick chestnut colored hair and a white man's swagger, which she found off putting. He draped his arm across the waitress's shoulder and said in a jocular tone.

"My girl tells me you are stranded for the night. We'll put you up at our place and then we'll get your car going in the morning. Little Bro here is a shade tree mechanic. If it can be fixed, he can do it." Then he turned a bright-eyed gaze on Hope, "You don't remember me. We met a few years ago, when I was at Fairleigh Dickerson, and you were at Rutgers. For a while, you dated a student there that I knew."

Hope had briefly dated a guy named David at Fairleigh Dickerson. He'd transferred to Syracuse where he was from because his mother was ill, and he wanted to be closer to help out. She nodded in acknowledgement that she had been on and off the campus for a brief time.

She said, "You must have a good memory because I was only on that campus a couple of times before he transferred to Syracuse University."

He leered at her and smiled, "Hey, you're hard to forget plus he talked about you in glowing terms."

Hope had gone to visit David a couple of times in Syracuse. Although they really liked each other, there was too much on both of their plates to sustain a long-distance romance. They'd parted as friends. She had no intentions of explaining anything to this stranger, who acted like they were long lost buddies, and he knew her.

"What's your name? I don't think you told us," she switched it up on him.

"Quinton Wickham, call me Wick. Some people call me Quick Wick."

Okay, Hope thought, as she racked her brain to try to find this guy in a passing scene from her college days. He didn't register. She could only remember meeting and hanging out with two of David's friend. Wick wasn't one of them. She didn't remember ever seeing the guy. She was known in her family for her recall power, so this was not like her to forget a face, a name maybe, but with his unusual one and ways, not likely. Hope and David had been an interracial couple so no telling who were watching them.

"You're sure we actually met in New Jersey?" Hope asked skeptically.

"It may have been at a distance. Yea, I'm sure," he snickered and winked at her.

They went to Annoa's house, the kind eyed waitress. Hope was uncomfortable in Wick's presence all evening but fascinated to sit with everyone and hear about Annoa's family history. Her family was old haole/ Hawaiian, known as Kama'aina. Her mother, who now lived in Kona, was born in this house. It was a beautiful, spacious home with Hawaiian art, feather works known as kahili, quilts, and Koa wood furniture. Koa wood is rich, warm, and stunning. Koa is a wood that only grows in Hawaii so although some of the décor was shabbily chic, the house had an air of natural polished finery.

They all drank several bottles of the Hawaiian beer, Primo, while deciding on a plan for retrieving the vehicle the next day. Hope was not used to guzzling so much beer so by the time they all staggered off to their assigned rooms to sleep, she wasn't sure what was going to happen the next day. She only knew that she needed to sleep it off because it had been a long, strange day. Hope had been given a small bedroom with a single bed with a tiny nightstand. Deana and Godwin were down the hall in a larger room and the guy Annoa called, "Brah-la" went out to an ohana, a small guest house, on the property. Wick and Annoa had their bedroom in an upstairs suite.

Hope's plan for a deep sleep was thwarted by the sound of fierce sexual activity above her head. She finally placed the pillow over her head and buried herself under the ample Hawaiian quilts before she could fall asleep. Hope couldn't wait to get away from this scene. She loved the tranquility the home gave off, but Wick's presence was a bit toxic for her. She liked Annoa. Because he seemed a bit too familiar with his approach toward her, Wick rubbed Hope the wrong way. However, she woke refreshed, with not much of a residual hangover from the previous night's guzzled Primo beer and smoked Kona Gold.

The quiet house seemed deserted as she freshened up in the nearby bathroom, put on the previous day's outfit with a touch of essential oil for good measure, tidied the bed and wandered toward the distinct smell of Kona coffee in the kitchen. There she found brewed coffee and a note from Deana saying they would be back to pick her up after they got the car situation handled. Hope assumed they had all left together. She wandered out to the back lanai and settled in with a steaming hot cup of coffee and a piece of fruit. The lanai faced a hilly orchard of fragrant guava trees and Hope relaxed in the welcoming morning sunshine. The ringing telephone snapped her out of her doze. Not sure if she should answer in someone else's house or where the phone was located, she just sat there before the ringing stopped. She tried to relax again, but wondered if Deana was trying to reach her. Well, she had no car so she couldn't go anywhere. She may as well relax She heard footsteps and turned to see Wick padding barefooted out towards her.

"Mornin' darlin'! That was Godwin calling. When they got to their car it was covered in Pele's Hair, so it is going to be a mess for Brah- la to get it towed and fixed. They're at the Volcano House with Anno'," he dropped the 'a' when he said her name.

Hope looked at him blankly and he started laughing. She wasn't sure what was funny. She was feeling uncomfortable with him again and not sure what his response meant. She had an acute unpleasant jolt of realization that she was stuck here with him alone.

"Oh, you have probably never seen Pele's Hair since this is your first visit to the Volcano. That stuff is amazing to see, but it can do some damage. Tumbleweeds of Pele's Hair can collect on Saddle Road where you all broke down. Pele's Hair can be more than 3 feet long and are often less than 0.04 inches thick. Pele's Hair form when molten lava is torn apart. Like the thinning strings that form when you pull your hands away from sticky dough, the hair strands form when blobs of lava are torn apart and the fluid lava still connecting them is stretched thin. It is rock that's like the thinnest of glass and breaks into the tiniest pieces if handled the wrong way. Pele's Hair only form on basaltic volcanoes that produce fluid lava like in Hawaii. However, if the melted rock is too fluid, it will behave more like water and form droplets instead. In Hawaii those are known as Pele's Tears. Hawaii is the only place you see this side of Mother Nature."

"How did you end up living here, all the way from New Jersey? Were you studying geology, or do you have family here?" Since he seemed to be enjoying playing tour guide and teacher, Hope decided to probe for information.

"No, no family or degree," he laughed and shook his head. "The military drafted me when a few bad grades left me flunking out of college. They sent me here on the last leg of my tour after a stint in Vietnam. My mother was dying of cancer, so I was R&R-ing here as my last stop before transitioning back to the mainland. A couple of my Army buddies wanted to tour the Big Island, so I figured I'd take a couple of days and hang out before going back to Jersey. I met Anno' on my first day here. As a matter of fact, I met her at Akamai Barnes, while listening to Ted's band. As it turned out, my mother died while I was actually en route to Hawaii. Not one of my uncles tried to reach me so when I called home to let my Mom know I was on my way, that's when I found out that they had cremated her without letting her only child know what was happening. Well, needless to say that had I gone back to Jersey, there would have been hell to pay. Anno' took pity on me in my grief and now here I am, living off the land!" He said that as he stretched his blue jeaned legs into the sun and put his hands behind his head with a smirk on his face.

Hope had almost started to feel some humanity from him until he started acting like the cat that swallowed the canary. Her hackles jumped back up again when she looked at him and saw what could only be described as lustful hunger. She was not happy being left alone at this isolated house with this man.

"We're going to pick up Deana and Godwin. Anno' is working and Brah-la has to get a tow truck. Are you ready to go?" Hope affirmatively nodded her head in relief.

Chapter 7

Chiefs of the Trinity

Kolohe

I came back to the here and now when Chez, who was tethered in the back of the truck, started barking ferociously, as we turned down our long driveway. I checked the rear view mirror and she was on my side, peering intently ahead. All I saw was what appeared to be a long branch in the long winding drive ahead. However, as I slowed and we drew closer, I realized it was a huge timber rattler across the drive coming from the stream moving towards the tree line up the hill. It was so big that I could see its eyes. The snake looked right at us, scared the daylights out of me and silenced Chez's barking. It was slow, had a malevolent look and appeared to be bloated, which I concluded it must be impregnated. This was a little early in the year for these creatures to be out and reproducing. This was the biggest timber rattler, I have ever seen. We don't usually see any because they are illusive and avoid people.

I was afraid I'd hit it with my truck and didn't like that idea with Chez in the back so I started revving my engine in hopes that the vibration would send the sluggish thing on its way. It seemed to leisurely slide up the hill towards the trees. When it got to the first tree, the thing actually turned around and looked at us, as if daring us to come after it. I immediately took off just in case it was thinking of jumping in the truck after Chez. Its behavior was just that bizarre. I didn't have a lot of knowledge about the species. My son liked to study them and a friend who is a CP Forester had discussed it with all of us during one of the Stewardship Training Programs that I'd sponsored for the community at the Fire Hall.

In any case, the sense of something "kolohe" or lethal crossing my path was not a good feeling. The Hawaiian word came to mind first because just that brief encounter with the rattler gave me a flashback to what I'd just been meditating on and really reliving as I drove across the mountain. Seeing an old acquaintance from my past Big Island days really put me in somewhat of a strange state of mind. My experiences there had shaped and affected a substantial portion of my life, some of it for the good and some not.

I'm a big believer and observer of symbolism so I took this huge snake manifestation as a sign that I should proceed with extreme caution on the whole "Carpenter Situation", as some of us, like Head Chief Jesse and Attorney Graham, had started calling it. We had weaved a very delicate balance of community agreements and every little detail had to be attended to for it not to fall apart. We were dealing with a lot of loot and some deep karmic ties, so it was a bit scary. The Wintu could balk and call the gold their heritage; the Dixon family could make an 'inheritor's' claim; Carpenter could change his mind and say 'finders keepers'; the courts could end up being involved, etc. Jesse and Graham were sure that we were well down the road to settling the conundrum and they might very well be correct in their assessment, but that snake appearance slowed my roll.

I realized that much of the success of this mission depended on Joanie keeping Carpenter together because he could be very jumpy and irrational. Graham had an idea of how skittish that man could be, but neither of us wanted to worry Jesse with it. Although, Head Chief had dealt with all types, so I really don't think we are pulling the wool over his eyes. He was an astute guy and Carpenter was pretty transparent, so it didn't take a lot of interaction for a keen observer like Jesse to figure him out.

When I got to the house, Pete was hitting golf balls off of his custom-built practice tee out on the hillside near our log cabin. I told him about the big rattler and my sense that it was a cautionary sign. He laughed and reminded me that our fire crew and other staff had been doing a lot of roadside fuel reduction work to remove flammable vegetation and create fuel breaks, as part of our Fire Department's fire prevention stewardship project. His take was that "White Jesse" (Pete's nickname for Head Chief because of his white hair) had factored in the cautionary concerns and taken all of it into consideration before he accepted our proposal for a plan of action. Pete's master's degree was in Organizational Management, and he was really well trained at setting aside emotions and doing straight circumstantial analysis. I sometimes felt that he could be somewhat dismissive of my hard-earned intuitive abilities. However, to be fair, that was not all of the time with Pete. He often listened to my sensitivities as to which way the "wind was blowing", as he called it.

As he was hitting practice balls off his tee box, we kicked around my thoughts on the oddness of the fact that I'd known the Dixon man's sister from Hawaii, of all places.

When we started discussing karmic lines, I heard my mother come out and sit on the front deck. Chez was already out of the truck, had taken care of her business, quenched her thirst from her well-water bucket, so as soon as she heard Momma out on the deck, she abandoned Pete and me for more interesting company. My mother walked to the edge of the deck and asked me what happened. I went over, sat down, and gave her a quick thumbnail of how the situation was progressing.

She said, "I've been thinking about your question on what I remember of my great-grandparents. More memories than I thought I had have started to come to mind.

The most I remember about GG Mule was his reputation. He became head Deacon at the family church, Hardy Grove. After that, a member of our family was head Deacon until this very day. I can recall quite a bit about the Deacon line of secession. Great-Grand Daddy was the first one from our family to head up the Deacon Board. When GG Mule died, my Grand Daddy Dee was voted to be the next head of the Deacon Board.

He died of the plague in 1925, when my brother was a baby, before my birth. Uncle Clay was voted to the post because the congregation really wanted men who had their own land and understood what our farmers were going through to stay on the farm and raise a family. Many of the preachers were not actual farmers so it was important to the women of the congregation that the Deacons, who made the operating decisions for the church, owned their own farms. As you know, there is a long and historical reason for this attitude. Anyway, Uncle Clay was Grand Daddy Dee's brother.

Evidently, he was a very successful farmer. His wife, Bertha, was a smart enterprising woman who turned everything she could into a plus for her family. She and my Grandma Sarah were close. I remember going out to their farm for the big family gatherings with lots of really good food and fun for all us cousins who enjoyed each others' company. Uncle Clay was hurt really bad on a piece of farm equipment that he was trying out and he could hardly walk so he'd sit on the porch and sing. He had a beautiful voice, and his boys took after him. Bertha got the idea of them going around doing church concerts for donations so they'd put Uncle Clay in an old wooden wheelchair, which gave them a sympathy factor, and he would lead those boys of his in revival-style concerts at the different black churches around North Carolina and even some schools.

Aunt Bertha and her daughters could sew anything. She made them custom outfits, so they looked very professional. They became very popular and called themselves the Henderson Barbershop Quartet. One of the sons even opened a barbershop that he had for many years. They came to Durham to St. John's Baptist Church when Lee was our Director of the Youth Choir and put on a concert for us to raise money for our robes.

That wasn't the only time I saw them perform either. They were on the program at Hillside High School when I was a student there. It made me very proud, but by the time they came to my high school, Uncle Clay was not able to travel anymore. It was only the sons, but still really good musically. The sons seemed to enjoy continuing the legacy. Aunt Ora's husband became Head Deacon after Uncle Clay couldn't walk anymore."

My mother astounded me as she shared her ancestral memories of family history. I wanted to hear more. She obliged me as we prepared dinner, sat, and ate together. There was a lot to tell. We talked into the night. Pete was fascinated too and stayed up to listen. Momma was enjoying holding the floor because, like Pete, she was an early riser, so for her to stay up late sipping her hot tea while we sipped our wine was a real treat. She had never explored these stories with me. Momma said she just assumed I knew much of this history and family stories from always being around the old folks, like GG Skinner, her grandmother, her father, and Aunt Lee.

"Now, you know that crazy G-Boy, JRG, is the Head Deacon nowadays," Pete and I laughed at her nickname for her first cousin, who we always enjoyed for his humorous accounts of the family history and life, especially the church gossip.

She told us much of what she could remember about the family and the Deacons of Hardy Grove. Pete was held as rapt as I, since he came from a long line of ministers, preachers, and evangelists. Church and community culture always held his interest.

Karmic connections, like bloodlines, were fascinating to me so I loved hearing these interwoven tales of life's patchwork that my mother was pulling out of her memory bank.

We were transported back to the times of our forefathers by my mother's telling.

Chapter 8

DEACONS OF HARDY'S GROVE

History

125 Years in a Black Southern Country Church

Deacon Mule Skinner:

Southern slavery ended in 1865 with the passing of the momentous 13th Amendment. One of the developments during the remainder of the century was the solidification of the black Christian church. Most of the rural black Christians of that day only met intermittently for outdoor camp meetings, when itinerate preachers would travel into the community by foot, horseback, or buggy. These camp meetings were an off shoot of the slavery times when black Christians met to have their own secret worship services that could be enjoyed in their own fashion, away from white overseers.

Here was the origin of Hardy Grove Baptist Church. During the time of Reconstruction, some blacks ("coloreds") were able to acquire their own land. Mr. Henry Wilson in Granville County, North Carolina managed (through hook and, some say, crook) to amass and keep up the taxes on over 1000 acres, an unheard-of accomplishment in those days. Hardy's Grove was part of his property holdings that he had acquired. Mr. Hardy's family insisted that the deal include land for the church community. He attended the camp services and offered the grove as a building site because he knew that some of the women complained about not having decent, "civilized" facilities.

The location was ideal because everyone in this remote community knew the site and there was already a colored cemetery near the grove.

In 1893, the men of the community put their heads together and set a building plan. They wanted to build a small modest façade. Some of the men who considered themselves the "Founding Deacons" were encouraged by old Mule Skinner to "put up something that will make the church Missionary Mothers proud". Mule was well respected by the other men because he'd been a Buffalo Soldier who'd travelled all out west and lived to get back to tell the tale. He was also part Cherokee, and many thought he had a mysterious connection to the land they stood on.

Mule's wife, Alice - he called her Al, was a Missionary Mother, even though, some of the ladies thought she was a little too independent for the "position", as she ran a roadside "store", which was more of a large, enclosed vegetable stand, for the harvest from her sumptuous vegetable gardens. Now, Al secretly thought of herself as a businesswoman, but always kept the farmer persona publicly. However, some of women still cast a side eye at her as being different. She figured that no amount of acting humble would change their minds because they knew she had parlayed what little she came out of slavery with into some semblance of financial independence.

Mule had helped all he could while he was gone on his "walkabout", which is how she referred to his travels for first one thing and then another. They'd met while she was still a young slave and he worked for a trading ship captain. The ship sailed up and down the east coast picking up goods and then docked back on the Carolina coast during bad sailing months. They'd come inland with a wagon full of goods to sell at the plantations. Mule was never a slave because his mother was Cherokee, so he got paid for his labors, although they were what Mule called "slave wages". Al has had to remind him on a number of occasions that he sounded ridiculous using that expression, especially to a former slave, because she never saw any parts of those wages. He always just laughed her off like she'd told a great joke.

His happy-go-lucky ways attracted her to him. Those same ways had also been a source of tension in their marriage because she was the opposite when it came to life's chores and burdens. While she enjoyed a good laugh, she was deadly serious about the practical things in life so sometimes she had to poke a hole in his bubble. However, one thing she never wanted to do was make him feel tied down, after all when you marry a sailor, it's not the same as marrying a farmer.

She's a farmer and a darn good one. Mule was an adventurer which is how he ended up as one of those Buffalo Soldiers and being out west for years, which meant that she had to fend for herself and their kids. Sometimes she didn't know if he was dead or alive. Well, he was back now and seemed like he didn't want to travel anymore. He even stood for Deacon at the church. He said what began to interest him in organized religion was his experience of trying to make it back from the western front, after his soldiering days were over. The Chautauqua helped him get back home to her through their different camps that spread across the country.

At first, Al thought Mule was talking about his mother's people, as he slowly opened up to her about his long, complex journey home from the 'Pacific Coast' as he called it, she learned that the Chautauqua are old Methodists, revivalists, educators, artists, performers, and idealists who have set up schools and camps for those they call Seekers. The Chautauqua brought in entertainment and culture for the whole community, with speakers, teachers, musicians, showmen, preachers, and specialists of the day. Al was a little skeptical of the Methodist, but their oldest daughter, Sarah liked them because they created schools of higher learning for colored people and Sarah always had her nose stuck in the bible, or any book she could get her hands on. Al had to go along with it to keep the peace.

Mule had met and connected with several of the western native peoples. He'd learned their tribal languages and customs along the way. This helped him accept his own heritage and deal with the tragedies that had befallen his mother's people. He was mostly treated as a black man, so he accepted that too, especially after he married Al. It felt good to be back with his wife and own family and community. He wanted to contribute so he applied to be a church Deacon and was accepted. Now they needed to get busy building the church sanctuary. He was getting old, and he wanted to see the church go up in his lifetime. Mule knew that they would need more help than they had now to get this church built so he had plans.

His plans eventually came to fruition and from then on other men in the family took up Deaconship and helped keep Hardy Grove Baptist Church alive and well as a place of worship, community, and comfort, as he'd hoped.

Deacon DeWitt Henderson:

It had been a long journey. DeWitt instantly felt that he was home when he crossed the Granville County line. It was his first time here, but he felt a quickening in his spirit, like here was his destiny. He knew this wasn't just all about intuition. He had taken this detour in his journey for a specific reason and her name was Sister Sarah Skinner. He'd met her while he was in Raleigh taking a study course for lay ministers at Shaw University. She was quietly unimposing, yet you couldn't help but notice her because of a certain kind of intensity in her posture and eyes. Then she spoke at one of the classes that he attended, and he was a goner. Her diction was perfect, and her voice tones were so soothing and modulating that he closed his eyes to listen. She knew her what she was talking about on the somewhat esoteric biblical subject matter that was being discussed, hermeneutics.[2] He couldn't get enough of talking to her. She was a true teacher. Sarah was quiet, not shy, just soothing.

She seemed to know things before he knew, so one day she asked him, "Well, are you going to hook up that buggy and ride over to

Granville County to talk to Mule and Al?"

When he looked shocked, she just laughed under her breath until her shoulders were shaking with mirth. His course was over in two weeks so he told her that he would go back home near Charlotte first, and tell his Daddy that he was going to get married. The family always had advice on how things should go in life and DeWitt knew that they would have something to say about this too. He was pleasantly surprised when she agreed. Then really astonished when he got back home, and his brother Clay said that he knew they were giving land lotteries in Granville County and that they should each apply for one. If they came through, he would be willing to move too. They'd applied and both of them were accepted! Here he was, many months later on his way to take a look at the land. He still had to meet Sarah's parents in person. He had written them twice and now they knew that he was serious about their daughter.

'Dee' (as his family called him) and his brother Clay wasted no time building their small, comfortable houses. Planting season would be upon them shortly. They both had a lot to accomplish in a short time. Clay had married his hometown girl before he left and had to get her moved to his farm.

Dee and Sarah received her parents' blessings to marry, especially when they found out that he had practical skills. They were concerned that because they had met at the University, he might have his head in the clouds. He quickly dispelled that notion when he told them about the land he had secured and the house he was building. It was official. They would marry after planting season. She was now certified to teach and planned to have classes at their church once it was built. Mule was determined to have the church built by Christmas, even though Dee wasn't sure how this was going to get done because they all had busy schedules, with building, planting, and harvesting.

Mule had been busy writing to various groups that he had interactions with during his travels (or 'walkabouts' as Al called them). He'd received generous donations and support from a number of organizations, so he announced at a Deacon Board meeting at his house that they had the money for the building materials and now he wanted time commitments from each of the men in the community, if only a few hours a week. This really put the pressure on Dee because he had a lot to do to shape up his place. Once everyone started talking about their own needs and how they could accomplish both keeping their farms going and getting the church up, they came to agreements to help each other. It made Dee and Clay feel more at home in the community and Mule treated them like sons. Mule had two daughters, so Dee felt purposeful marrying into this family.

The church went up surprisingly fast because Mule had raised enough money to pay for all the materials. Two or three men worked at the building site a couple of hours during the week. They all came prepared to work on Sunday. After the morning service, they would all work for most of the afternoon, while the women set up table boards of food that they had preprared. Everyone would sit down together for dinner. It felt like family and the project went along well. They were ready to occupy the building by Thanksgiving. Sarah and Dee were married on that Thanksgiving with the christening of the church. Sarah was proud to be the first bride to marry in the church building and she looked so petite and delicate that everyone audibly caught their breath when Mule proudly strutted her down the aisle. Mother Alice, as he now called Sarah's mother, was playing the organ that she had donated to the church. She said it would get more use at the church than at home, now that her daughters were both going to be married. Nora, Sarah's sister, was her Matron of Honor and Clay was his Best Man. He was impressed with the way the women here toiled alongside their men. The men bragged that their wives got up before dawn, had hot breakfast ready, then worked in the field all day until time to cook a sumptuous supper. Mother Alice had a huge garden, plenty of chickens, a sow with piglets, mules and, of course, a cow. They didn't cash-farm tobacco anymore because Mule was too old and had some sort of government pension from his days with the Buffalo Soldiers. Most of the men had to farm a cash crop, so Mule was fortunate to have a prosperous situation with his wife's little store selling her garden items.

Dee looked at his delicate little bride and wondered how she would be able to bear the burden of a farmer's wife. She may have grown up on a farm, but she was really a teacher, a deep thinker and very spiritual woman. As he gazed at her, he wondered how he could protect her from some of life's harsh realities. He felt as though she should be cloistered and remain untouched by him or life. When she lifted his hand to put the little thin ring on it, all he could think of was touching her most intimate parts with that finger. He knew, if necessary, he would work himself to death to keep her happy.

Deacon Garland Hedgely:

Garland rolled to a sitting position from his bed and looked around at the little one room cabin. Everything was a mess. Since his wife died, he had a hard time getting anything done. He supposed it was the grief. Truth be told, he was exhausted from taking care of her during her illness and trying to work his land at the same time. He wasn't really young anymore. He was a middle-aged widow now with no children or wife to help him. The land that he had managed to hang on to might be up for grabs now from the county tax man. With this plague sweeping through, killing so many people, the tax collector couldn't keep up with who was alive and who was dead. He knew he needed to pay, yet he hadn't produced enough of a cash crop to do it. He not only feared he would lose his land, but now that his wife was gone, he wasn't sure if he even cared. He felt like Job in the bible.

Garland was standing in his yard, throwing out scraps for the chickens when he heard the wagon on his road. He saw Clay Henderson, one of the church Deacons coming.

"Good Sunday, Mr. Hedgely," he called as he hopped off the buggy and reached in for a cloth covered basket. "I just came from the church, and it was announced that your wife passed last month. My Bertha sent over some Sunday supper for you. Plus, I wanted to let you know the news that my brother Dee passed away this past Wednesday. Lord knows we need His mercy. This plague is taking so many good people and sickening others so bad that they can't work."

Clay had been a good friend to Garland, even letting a couple of his sons help him at harvest season. He thanked him and offered him a rocking chair on the little porch that his wife had insisted she needed to shell her garden peas. 'Hedge' sat down on a wooden soda box. He looked in the basket and his mouth started to water. Bertha Henderson was known for her cooking skills, and he realized that he was hungry because he was living mostly off of coffee and eggs for the past month. He listened politely as Clay, who was a talkative man, brought him up to date on the community happenings. His ears did perk up a little when he talked about his niece, his brother's oldest daughter, who was back home from a college for the blind to help her mother through these tough times. He remembered the tall thin girl. She was striking with her long neck and smooth brown skin. She wore thick, thick eyeglasses, but it didn't detract from the intelligent expression and high cheek bones. His dead wife was beautiful and smart. He liked a smart woman. He knew he needed a woman around this place. How could he ask someone else to share this one room hut, especially one who was nearly blind. Anyway, he was close to losing the farm and older, so what would he have to offer a lady.

Clay invited him to come back to church next month when they were having a traveling evangelist preaching. They were only holding church once a month now because of the plague so he promised he would. He wanted to ask Clay some more about his niece. He remembered her name as Ora, but he was hungry and wanted to eat the food that Bertha had sent. He knew that Clay would go on and on if he encouraged him, so he stood and pretended to be about to start cutting some wood in the woodpile next to the door.

Clay caught the hint and said, "Well, I reckon I'd better get on back home and let Bertha know that you're alright."

"Thank her for the supper basket. I'll return the basket to church next month. I'm sorry to hear about your brother. I hope his family will be well," Hedge managed to sound civilized, but he didn't want to get Clay going again.

Clay replied as he was climbing onto the buggy, "They'll be alright. He has three sons who are old enough to work the land and now Sarah has help from her oldest daughter, Ora. She might be legally blind, but she can see good enough to help around the house and keep her mother company through these trying times. She's very skilled at farming even with her lack of sight."

For some reason, Clay's visit gave Hedge a lift to his spirit, and he spent the next month using his time wisely around his farm. He cleared a small field for an orchard and used the trees to make boards with his small sawmill for an addition that he added to the house, so it had a separate kitchen next to the well on what was now the back porch. He'd changed the orientation of the house and put a wide front porch off the bedroom. Hedge felt an urgency about his tasks even though he hadn't teased out why, in his mind. At least he was getting out of his depression and giving the mules a much-needed work out.

Hedge tried to clean himself up for church and he thought he looked somewhat respectable when he arrived. However, as soon as he saw Ora with her mother and oldest brother, Andrew, driving up in his car, he felt untidy and uncertain of himself. He gave himself a little talk about being a hard-working landowner. The self pep talk worked, so when they came into the church, he walked over to Mother Henderson and offered his condolences on the loss of her husband. She was gracious and polite but seemed unfocused and understandably distracted. The young Deacon Henderson shook his hand, took him by the elbow, led him a few steps away while Ora and her mother took their seats.

"Mama is still coming to terms with our loss, so I know you understand. We were sorry to hear about your wife some months back as well. Uncle Clay has been keeping us up on how everyone in the community is doing during this plague. I know you know it has been real tough for all of us. My Daisy won't let the children leave the farm. They are so young," he confided quietly.

Hedge thought there was no time like the present, so he ventured to the young Deacon, "Mr. Andrew, I don't want to overstep my place here, but life moves pretty fast, as you well know by now. I'm a farmer with my own land and I just built on some improvements to my house and doing all I can to keep things up. A man in my position needs a wife and help mate. Would it be offensive to y'all if I called on your sister, Ora?

The young Deacon looked surprised, "You know she is legally blind, right? However, she has some sight and the school she attended taught her how to read Braille and adjust to her problem seeing. She gets things done around our place fairly easily and she helps my mother quite a bit."

"Frankly, Mr. Andrew, your sister seems quite capable and strong to me. If she will allow me to call on her, I'd be grateful. You know I'm a bit older than she is and not a real educated man, even though, I get by alright with the help of the Lord," Hedge replied sincerely.

"Yes sir, I will speak on your behalf to Sis and the family." He slapped him on the back in a congenial fashion and Hedge immediately felt like family, so he knew he had a good person on his side already.

Hedge was never a social person, but Sunday service and the Supper afterwards that the ladies served just lifted his spirits. He even got to tell Ora how much he enjoyed her dish of gravy smothered rabbit and noticed that she blushed a little in her own subdued way and quietly replied,

"Why thank you, Mr. Hedgely, glad you enjoyed it."

For some reason, this little response from her set off his imagination and he had to walk away and light his pipe because his mind already had her in bed with him making love. He simply knew this young woman was going to be his wife and they would make a life together.

Hedge and Ora were married a year after her father passed away and a little over a year after Hedge had become a widower. "Sis", as he'd taken to calling her like all the rest of her family, always called him "Mr. Hedgely". She was a hard worker and could cook anything like nobody's business. They had two strapping boys, a pretty little girl, who was the apple of his eye, and built up his farm to prosperity. She told him that it was out of respect, and that made him smile every time he thought about her while they made love, moaning his name, "Oh, Mr. Hedgely".

Their marriage was happy and satisfying for both of them. They made a good team. Since his family lived so much further south, they spent a lot of time with her family and her mother stayed with them all the time after their children were born, which was a big help.

Deacon Andrew Henderson

Andrew couldn't believe it. Life was getting harder and harder for him. First, his father died and left things with the farm in bad shape. He had to struggle to pay back taxes because his mother was a great teacher, but she didn't care about the business side of things. That left him as the oldest child and son to figure things out.

Now, his wife had another miscarriage and was barely getting around. His sister was pregnant and not married. Rosellee won't say who the boy is because she "doesn't want to get him in trouble". His mother is blaming him for not "keeping an eye" on her, which he considered unfair.

They were keeping her home, not allowing her to go to church or anywhere else until they decided what to do and which boy it was. "Lee", as they called his sister, was always feisty and a hand full so this was just the next stage in her rebellion, as he saw it. His sister, Ora, wanted her to come live out at her farm with their mother.   He needed Lee home to help take care of his children with his wife so ill.

His brother Charles married the "love of his life", who just happened to have inherited quite a large farm when her father and half her family were taken by the plague. His brother, Lang, had joined the Army as soon as he found out they were taking colored soldiers, so he had no help on the farm.

His youngest sister was about to be married, a little too soon if you ask him. His mother seemed to go along with the match, and he was not able to do anything about it. He complained to his grandmother who always took his side against her daughter, for all the good that did them.

Lee was still strong and tried to help out some in the barn, tying tobacco leaves; but she was pregnant plus had his children to contend with whenever his wife had one of her "spells". His two oldest had started school. The youngest, Alicia, was always under foot and into everything.

He didn't know how much more he could take. He had to get this crop in, so he could have some cash money for the family. He trudged along behind the mule hitched to the tobacco sled and tried to contemplate what he would do if he couldn't keep up the farming. His wife's cousin, Ely Marble, had let his oldest son, Willie, come help him out for several days at a time. The boy really should be either in school or helping his father and younger brother on their own farm. It was good to have him though because he was young, strong, and always had jokes to crack. They got along well. He and the kid enjoyed each others' company. They worked hard and shared a lot of laughs together. It helped ease the burden to have some support from the family. Today, though, Willie was back home, and he was working alone. Lee said she was going to go down to the barns and start stringing the harvested leaves. She had fast hands, but couldn't lift the heavy wooden stick poles that the tobacco was tied to because she was pregnant.

This was the last sled load of leaves, so at least he had harvested all the tobacco. He would turn the fields over with the plow after he got the all the leaves 'strung and hung' for curing.

He carefully guided Nell, the half blind mule pulling the sled, into the barn opening by making clicking sounds with his mouth. As soon as Nell stopped, the mule made a loud whinny. Old Nell was blind, but the mule seemed to always know when it was quitting time.

"Okay, give me a minute to unhook the sled!" he yelled.

"Well, if it isn't the talking mule! Nell, I guess he understood what you said, which is good because Deacon Stubborn-As-A-Mule doesn't listen to anybody else," Lee guffawed as her hands rapidly and repeatedly twined the tobacco stems into a bunch and attached them to the horizontal posts. The big spool of twine on the post at her shoulder was spinning like a top as she moved quickly and methodically. She was really skilled at this and did not break her pace at all as she looked at him and said, "Brother, you talk to that mule Nell like it's your wife. Well, I guess right now you do spend more time with Nell than your own wife."

He knew Lee loved his wife like a sister and she was probably voicing some complaint or other they had against him. He unhooked the guidelines on the heavy leather yoke from the sled, then went around and lifted it off the mule's shoulders and hung the whole contraption on its hooks near the barn opening. He led the mule out to the animal barn without saying a word to his sister. He knew that would make her even more hostile, so he was in for a rough afternoon, if she worked at the curing barns all day with him. He fed and watered Nell and went back to the little cubbyhole in this barn where he did paperwork for the farm. The children were not allowed in the animal barn.

It was nice and cool in here and smelled of fresh hay. He could also hear the brook just downhill from the barn bubbling. He had a small lunch box with some of last night's fried chicken, so he sat at his little table with its rickety chair and ate his chicken and biscuit with molasses in peace. He had a jug of well water, so he was able to just take a minute before going back to the back breaking work of lifting the poles to the upper part of the barn to start the 6-week curing process for the crop. One of the barns was already full and curing, but he just needed to get this other one ready to go as soon as possible. Timing was everything in properly curing tobacco, so they only had a matter of days to get the rest of the crop done. It could go quickly if Lee kept helping.

He knew this was not a good time to antagonize Lee so he really needed to muster all the patience he could, and the Lord would give him to handle these next few days of hard labor and family discord. Andrew considered himself a man who thought deeply about things. Even if he didn't always have the correct answers, he still liked to have a plan before a crisis hit. Right now, his only plan was to try to keep the peace for the next few days until he could finish getting this tobacco crop in and the source of cash that he desperately needed. He could not let his sister goad him into an argument. He could see that Lee was spoiling for a fight. As soon as he stepped foot in that barn, she was going to go after him, and she was pretty tough.

In fact, Lee was the only one of his siblings that scared him. His other sisters were much gentler in nature and his brothers, who were also younger than him, always bowed to him as the elder. Lee always challenged their father and now him. Everyone in the family referred to her as a "tough cookie". She was great with the children, and they all adored her, even when she exercised discipline, which consisted of a keen little tree switch on their legs. They would run, jump, and scream like the little switch was killing them. A few minutes later, they would be laughing about the whole thing and hanging on her lap. The thing the children seemed to hate the most was when she would make them go find their own switch for their punishment for misbehaving. They always cry and beg to keep from delivering their own form of torture. Lee would fold her arms, stand on the porch and sternly instruct them, "Better not break off some little twig or I'll get my own for your butt!"

As he trudged back to the curing barn, he felt like one of his own children looking through the bushes trying to find an acceptable switch for his punishment that he knew was coming. He furtively returned to the barn, then immediately went to the other side, and started hoisting the heavy poles of tobacco up to the ceiling in a simple process known as 'barning'. It was back breaking work, especially alone. Lee, who was skilled, quick, and methodical, had finished tying almost all the tobacco that he'd picked and hauled in.   His main purpose this afternoon was to get the poles in place and start the curing process. When he was nearly finished, he decided to take a break, and check with Lee to see how much was left to string. He didn't think there could be much more left, at least, he hoped there wasn't because he was bone tired.

He climbed down from the rafters of the barn, walked outside and expertly rolled a cigarette from the loose tobacco in his little white cotton draw string pouch. Andrew drew a couple deep drags on the neatly hand- rolled cigarette, stretched, and walked slowly around to the tying deck. He stopped dead in his tracks, stunned into paralysis for a moment. His sister was lying on the barn floor in a small pool of blood. He threw the cigarette in the dirt and ran to her side. She looked at him with the most helpless eyes he'd ever seen. Lee was frightened and so was Andrew. He wasn't sure where his strength came from, considering how tired he was from all the 'barning' work, but he managed to lift his big boned sister and run to the house with her in his arms. He burst in the house calling his wife's name. He took Lee upstairs to her room and put her on the bed.

His wife took over because, even in her weakened state, she knew a miscarriage when she saw one. She, herself, had suffered three of them so Andrew got out of her way and just followed any instructions she gave him. Andrew knew he needed to go get his wife some assistance.   He helped with fetching towels, water and whatever else he was instructed to do. Little Alice refused to leave Lee's bedside. When the two older children came in from school, he put them in the family car and drove as fast as he could safely go to his sister Ora's house to get his mother. They left the two children with Ora and rushed back home in time to see his exhausted wife staggering out of Lee's room with a small bloody bundle. The baby was not stillborn. The infant had died after a few halting cries, his wife told them.

He could hear Lee screaming for her baby and little Alicia crying, "Here I am, here I am!" The entire scene was something out of nightmares. His mother told him to take the baby away and sent his wife to change her clothes and lie down. She put little Alicia to work helping get Lee cleaned up. Everyone knew that little Alicia liked to be helpful in a practical way so the tasks would calm her down. After an hour or so, his mother had things cleaned up including the dead baby. She washed and wrapped it in a large clean, soft, cotton flour sack. Andrew had stupidly put it in a bucket. He was not built for these kinds of emergencies. He took all the bloody towels out to the washhouse and put them in a barrel of water. He could do that much.

The family pulled together. His mother stayed with them, and the two older children stayed with Ora. He and his mother buried the poor little baby next to Andrew's father in the family burial plot on the farm. Since only the immediate family knew Lee was pregnant, there was no need to have an actual funeral. Lee and his wife were inconsolable. To lose a child after it had taken a breath was grievous to the women. When his wife had miscarried, she was never very far along in the pregnancies so there was no fully formed body to bury. There was a dark pall over the whole house. He wanted to take little Alicia out to his sister Ora's house. She refused to leave. She went between her aunt's room and her mother's, trying to console them. The only time, the child came downstairs to the kitchen was when her grandmother made her come eat her meal or told her she had a hot butter and molasses biscuit snack for her. He spent a lot of time at the barns, even though the leaves were all 'put up' and curing now. He kept busy as he could from sunrise to sunset. He came in for meals and his mother would have him take his wife up a tray. His mother took his sister up her food tray. This was necessary because every time Andrew came near Lee, she would start screaming some nonsense that it was his fault that she'd lost her baby.

The situation did not seem to be getting any better. His baby sister Zella, who was the sweetest and most gentle in the whole family, came back home; even though she had just quietly gotten married. Zella took little Alicia in hand and the two of them became inseparable. Zella brought a soothing spirit into the house and Lee started to perk up. His wife, though, seemed to be getting worse. One night she was so bad that he knew he had to get her to a doctor.   The next day he took her to Durham to see Dr. Weaver, the Negro doctor. The doctor was alarmed by her condition and admitted her to the hospital. Andrew stayed with his cousin Velma in Durham, who lived near the hospital. The next day, Dr. Weaver told him that his wife was too ill to go home He said he needed to observe and run some test to see what exactly was draining her strength. Andrew told him about the back-to-back miscarriages, which had happened at home They had not had the inclination nor money to bring her to Durham for medical care. No doctors in his town accepted Negro patients. Dr. Weaver told him there was nothing more Andrew could do right now. He advised to let her rest and to come back in three days. He would know more and have test results.

When Andrew got back to the farm, Lee was on her feet. It was pandemonium. Both Lee, his mother and little Alicia were inconsolable when they found out that he had left his wife in the hospital. He explained what the doctor said, so after much discussion, they decided that Lee would go over to Durham and monitor the situation while he caught up on the farming necessities. He wanted Alicia to go out to Ora's farm with his mother. The child raised such a stink, stomping around the house loudly and pitifully complaining that she was a motherless child, and nobody wanted her. It was so bad that his mother told Lee to take her to Durham, too. Alicia brightened after the arrangements were made for his sister Zella and her new husband to take them to Durham. Zella's husband had a house in town with a telephone. They were able to call their cousin Velma and she talked to Lee about living arrangements.

They decided that Lee could stay at Miz Pearl's across the street from Velma. She was a widow with a nice big house where she sometimes rented rooms to folks that she knew or their relatives and other Negro travelers, who found her in the Green Book. During the day, Alicia could play with Velma's younger children, while Lee was at the hospital; and sleep at Miz Pearl's at night.

Andrew knew he would have to pay. He still thought this was an acceptable situation considering that this was an emergency. He admitted that he was a little tight fisted with the money. Of course, that was because money was always in short supply.

He was going to have to get a job. He had started to hate farming and it wasn't bringing in enough money to sustain the whole family. He'd heard from one of the church deacons that the tobacco factory in town was hiring and he planned to go see about that job. Also, there was some hiring going on at Camp Butner. He wasn't sure if he could be that far away from the family and his land. However, it worked out, he had to bring in more income. The doctor and hospital bills were going to be hefty. He was close to losing the farm for back taxes, so he was going to have to find a way to either keep it or sell it and find another home for his family.

The world seemed to be going against him. He was a Negro man in a racist society so what else was new, he thought with more irony than bitterness. Andrew considered himself (and most folks agreed with him) a naturally cheerful, upbeat person so this very depressing situation went directly against his positive nature. Thinking this through, he decided that he would do everything he could to get back on his feet. He'd given Lee every extra cent he had in the kitchen jar for the stay in Durham, which seemed to satisfy her. He had enough for gas, so he'd gone to the factory. He knew the white foreman because he lived in the company's house next to the factory, over the tracks from the black part of town, in a two-story white clapboard house with a tiny front porch. Andrew's house was nicer than his, but that didn't matter. Andrew still had to come in his Sunday suit with his hat in hand and answer questions of the foreman if he wanted that floor manager's job. By the time he finished his bowing and scraping act, the guy was slapping him on his back and saying that Sheriff Cash was right, he was a good 'boy'. Andrew wanted to knock his head off. He sucked it up for the sake of getting the job and the money that he needed to take care of his family affairs. It was a pretty decent paying job and supervising a bunch of Negro women was easier than they thought when you'd known most of them your entire life. When he felt certain that he had the job secured, he drove back to Durham to see about his wife.

Dr. Weaver expected to release her from the hospital tomorrow and he wanted to make sure that he was there for that. All the way there, he fretted about her health, his children being scattered to family members, not being able to farm anymore and losing the family farm to taxes. He felt like Job, a story that his mother had made him read in the bible many times, during his days in her church school. She always said that we may not have a lot of books, but if we learn to read the bible, we can find the answers to life's dilemmas. Andrew had been raised by his mother and father to be a man of faith and that is what he would have to lean on now more than ever. With everything going on in his life, he felt a little guilty that he had not been able to do his due diligence on his deacon duties at Hardy Grove.

He knew that everyone there was praying for his wife. Even though, most of the deacons didn't have telephones at their homes, the word had gotten around by way of the "mule circuit". The farmers jokingly called it that because they would hitch up their mules to their flat bed wagons and ride to the local grange store, on the pretext of getting supplies. It was just as often a little time stolen from the hard work of farming to socialize with friends and get news of the community. They would stand around outside, pass a mason jar of Ely Marble's best corn liquor around and get caught up on whatever news they could glean. If it had been women, they would have called it gossiping. The men told themselves that it was tending to their community affairs. They usually didn't decide to do anything about a situation until they went home and discussed it with their women folk to find out from them what would be the best remedies or plan of action.

Andrew knew he'd need more help than ever when his wife came home so he had to trust that his community of women would have a plan to help him, and his family survive this crisis. He was certain that his mother would have thought things through, and she had a lot of wisdom, as well as faith.

When he arrived at the hospital, Lee was the first person he saw in the colored lobby because she was pitifully crying inconsolably. She saw him and ran into his arms wailing, "Brother, she's gone! Your wife is dead! My sweet friend was too good for this world! Lord have mercy on us!"

Chapter 9

Chiefs of the Trinity

Steller's

When Momma told the story of her mother's death, we all felt the fresh grief of that 5-year-old child. She stopped, as if choked up. Pete, sensing the strain of the telling, stood, and stretched. I was so touched that I was sort of paralyzed in place.

Pete said, "Let's get some rest. Hope, you've heard enough for tonight. You're both exhausted. You, Chief, still have some thinking on this 'Carpenter Situation' to do."

When I awoke the next morning to a sunny day and birds chirping, I looked out the window by our bed and saw a band of Steller's Jays, my favorite birds, out feeding in the yard. Pete must have thrown out feed for them because he loved them too. He said they looked like they were wearing tuxedos and top hats. The striking bird has a prominent black crest on its head and a generous long tail. The front of its body is usually black, and the color extends part way down its back with the wings and tail being a sparkling iridescent blue. This jay was named after the German naturalist, Georg Wilhelm Steller. Most people think they are called "Stellar" for their brilliant coloration, but it's spelled "Steller" for the person who documented their existence back in 1741.

We live at about 4,000 feet and that is the elevation that they really thrived in so our family of Stellers were alert, huge, healthy, and colorful. Chez had given up barking at them when they landed in the yard, because they just mimicked her bark right back at her.

She accepted them as part of the family or at least tolerable neighbors. Their arrival always put me in a good mood so I bounded out of bed, threw on a robe and went downstairs where I knew Pete would have coffee brewing. Pete's downstairs den/office doubled as a guest room. Momma was already up "piddling around", as she called it.

She loved to read her newspaper in the morning, the Miami Herald. Of course, we didn't have that, but she had somehow gotten a copy of the local town paper and was sitting at the kitchen table reading that and sipping her coffee. I grabbed a cup of steaming hot Kona and sat. The kitchen was bright with the morning sun because two of the walls were mostly made up of sliding doors that opened onto the wraparound deck. The kitchen table sat in between them. It was indoor/outdoor living at its best. It maximized our view of Dubakella Mountain, as Pete and I had planned when we designed the cabin.

"Pete went into town early this morning, got the newspaper and fresh pastries from that little place, Cathy's Caddie Cart. He also let the dog out and fed her. As you can see, he fed your yard birds too," Momma said pointing out the window at the Jays.

"Aren't the Jays beautiful? In his capacity as a consultant for SBA, he helped Cathy get a micro loan to start that little business, so he likes to support her. He must be out doing something in the powerhouse because I don't see Chez on the deck. She tends to follow him around when he's doing things outside on the property," I replied.

The phone rang just as I drained my cup and told Momma that I was going to go get dressed for the day. It was Head Chief White, who wanted to discuss the funeral for Dixon. I told him that I would call him back shortly because I'd had a late night and was getting a slow start. I just wanted to get my head on straight before I discussed that subject. It still felt sensitive to me. I was still digesting Momma's telling from last night. I just wanted to give myself time to catch up with myself, as Pete would sometimes advise me. Jesse seemed to understand and said he'd be in his office most of the day so call him when I could talk. I took my time to shower and dress before I called him back. As he tends to do, he launched right into the issue – the funeral.

"I want Carpenter there. You and Joanie make sure he sits with you two to show solidarity and that he is cleared of any major wrongdoing. You know him wearing a long beard doesn't endear him to the fire fighters. Many think he flaunts the rules just for doing that. I have defended him by saying he only drives the water tankers. It's not a funeral, but a memorial service. Bill Fischer at McDonald-Files has cremated the body and we've made the arrangements to use that facility for the memorial service. I've asked Joe Bower to speak mostly to lay groundwork for the buy-in on our program, which will dual-purpose us in squashing resistance now that we can source the funding. You know the social will has to be there to do collaborative work to learn what stewardship means and find the energy to carry the project all the way through. Our community's wildfire protection plan must be long term. At the same time, we have to take every opportunity to suppress fears that the Forest Service will come in and log the forest.

Joe's presence and support can help with that. Everyone trusts his monitoring and accountability efforts so that gives some built-in security to the collaborative."

Joe Bower was the founder of Citizens for Better Forestry and one of the area's foremost and respected conservationists. He and his wife Sue were Quakers.

They were a lovely couple, neighbors, and friends of mine, who always made sure that I had fresh organic vegetables from their extended gardens. The Bowers were invested in the success of the stewardship project and had worked with Jesse and me in a very key advisory capacity. Sue was an excellent communicator and had taught me so much about what to put in the full proposal that I wrote up for the project, even before we knew where the money would come from to launch it. I expressed to Jesse that I thought this was a smart move on his part to involve them. I wondered how Camilla would take it if she thought we were using her brother's demise for political reasons. Jesse said since I'd known her previously, he'd leave it up to me to explain our reasoning to her. Although, I wasn't comfortable with that, I agreed while reminding him that I had not seen her in over 30 years and only knew her for a relative short period then.

He rang off with, "I have complete confidence in your ability to smooth this situation with her."

I set about tracking Joanie down and talked to her about the service. She assured me that she would make sure that Carpenter went with us and behaved himself. He had a lot at stake here too. Jesse had given me Camilla's contact information and I planned to call her. I needed to make sure that I took the right approach, so I decided to get in a walk with Chez and spend some time at our "meditation" grotto. It was a beautiful day, and I needed some stress relief before I approached Camilla.

Momma decided to walk with us, despite the hills being challenging for her. When I told her about the memorial service becoming a bit political, she reminded me that everything is political. She was a veteran of the "hanging chad" disaster in Florida during the Bush/ Gore campaign. She said she learned the hard way, as an Election Manager, that everything from parking laws to voting machines was affected by politics. She suggested that I just be straight with Camilla and explain that there was a political element to the situation.

When we got back to the house, I called Camilla and told her that I would be on the Weaverville side of the mountain and wanted to have lunch with her if she was up to it. She readily agreed and said she would love to have a little time with me to catch up, as well. Camilla had always been a warm and positive person, so I felt more optimist of the outcome after speaking to her. We met at the Chinese restaurant in town, the only one for 75 miles. We chatted casually at first and laughed about the fact that you couldn't go two blocks in the Islands without running into a place that served Chinese food in some variety.

"How're you holding up," I asked to turn the conversation to the current situation.

"My brother and I only became close in the last few years, since his mother died. We have the same father who passed away quite a while ago. He came to Hawaii for a fresh start and then suddenly decided to move back to California and here of all places.

When we were kids, our mothers used to send us to our grandparents here in the summer. That's how we got to know each other. The rest of the year, we had no contact. Our mothers never got along so it was 'complicated'," she used finger quotes.

"Well, I want to talk to you about complications now as well," I launched in.

"A Fireman's Memorial is mostly honorific, but it's also political. Head Chief asked me to talk to you about the Program. Since we've known each other, he thought it would be best if you and I talked about it. There are some folks that he wants to add to the program who will be discussing things that have nothing to do with your brother or your lost. Being a Kama'aina, I know you understand the local people's concern for the land:

Ua Mau ke Ea o ka 'Āina i ka Pon," I said in my best Hawaiian.

"That's fine with me. Our grandparents are the only family that we had here, and they are gone. My son will not be able to make it because he's on assignment in China so it's only me. I'm really grateful that the Fire Chiefs are doing this. Hope, please will you reassure Head Chief Whyte that he can arrange the program anyway he sees fit. I trust he knows more than I do about all of this and frankly it's quite a burden lifted," she sighed.

"Thank you and you won't be disappointed. It's quite a community event when Firemen send off their fellow colleagues. Do you need help packing up his place?"

"He really didn't have much. A bunch of old maps, books, and some mining equipment. He seemed to be into rock hunting, but nothing too valuable. Although, I found documents that he seemed to be trying to obtain mining claims; no paperwork to indicate that he did so. I'm giving or throwing most of it away, except for old family photos. His life may have not been as fulfilled as he wanted it to be. There is not much I can do about it. He may have been trying to capture some of our childhood here. Our grandfather took him all around these mountains digging around or gold panning every summer. That was their thing together. I used to try to help, but it was not for this girl. Our grandmother and I would sometimes tag along to pick blueberries or fish."

"People still do a lot of gold panning and gemstone hunting here. O'Sullivan's is a business here is Weaverville that specializes in that sort of thing. They may know if your brother was trying to stake a claim somewhere. They're experts in this," I said, just as our delicious smelling food arrived, served by Queenie Lee herself.

Camilla looked sad thinking of her brother, so I changed the subject for relief.

"This is real Chinese food like you get in Hawaii. You know that Ms. Lee, her family, and the Chinese community here go all the way back to the 1800s. Did you ever visit the Joss House when you were a child? That's the Temple across the street from here. It's a State Park now because the Lee family wanted to preserve the legacy."

She shook her head no, as she expertly used the chop sticks to take an appreciative bite.

"Have you kept up with any of the Beach Mums?" I asked, using the name of our old Mom's group. It was our group's little joke combining beach bums and moms.

"Well, not closely, I know some of us are widows now. My Ron passed from cancer. I chose to stay in the house because I love living near the ocean. I had lost track of Jackie after Brah-la was killed in some sort of bar brawl. His cousin's husband tore down their house and built a small two-story apartment building there. It didn't go down well with the community in Puako, but we didn't have political chops to stop it. That side of his family was very well connected politically. I reached out to Jackie. She was very closed off. I didn't want to push it. I think she was closer to you during those Beach Mum days than me."

"Oh, my goodness, I didn't know any of this! When I separated from Doc and moved to Honolulu then to Florida, I didn't return for many years, when I was with my new husband, Pete, on vacation. I didn't try to look up anyone from my time with Doc."

I was really shocked to hear about all the deaths, especially about Brah-la, who was one of the halfway decent 'kanakas' that I met when I first moved to the Islands.

As we wrapped up our long, delicious lunch, based on my conversation with Camilla, it didn't seem prudent to tell her what her brother was really up to. I didn't think she would really want the complication. I knew she wasn't hurting for money because her husband, Ron, had been one of the most prosperous guys on the Big Island. He'd also had inherited family wealth. I was certain that she was very comfortable financially.

Although, I had some trepidation that she might think I was being devious for not telling her about the 'Carpenter Situation'. I was not going to make my job harder if I didn't have to right now. I was not asking for permission and hopefully forgiveness would not be necessary. We hugged and I promised to see her at the service. I drove away slowly as I thought of all the things we had discussed, especially what happened to Brah-la. As I drove back over the mountain, once again, I thought back to the circumstances when I first met him and members of his family on the Big Island.

Chapter 10

A Mighty Long Way

Lili

Doc and Godwin were the first people Hope met in Hawaii. They picked Deana and Hope up at the airport in Doc's sky-blue convertible Ford Falcon with cream leather interior. They draped them with two fragrant flower leis. Deana and Godwin were like teenagers together in the backseat. Doc was older than they were by about 20 years. He was charming in an old-world Hollywood kind of way. He was short and well built with thick dark curly hair. He looked like a Spanish matador. It turned out he was German.

When he started to help Hope into the car, he offered his hand with a bow and said, "Princess Lili, your chariot awaits."

Hope giggled and said, "Nice car."

His response threw her off, "Banality is beneath you, my Lili."

Hope thought, okay, this guy has a rap. She soon found out he was a brilliant Psychologist who'd moved here from Hollywood, so he also tended toward the dramatic.

They became fast friends. Even though, Hope had no romantic interest in him, he didn't feel the same. He told her that he'd fallen for her at first sight and came to visit nearly every day since she'd arrived. They really talked a lot. He was intellectually above her.

Hope used their time together as a learning opportunity. He'd lived an interesting life. She got him to talk about himself instead of him getting her to talk. His mother was a Jewess from Spain.[3] Doc's father was a German surgeon who'd opposed Hitler. His family lost everything when they fled for their lives and made their way to the United States before World War II broke out. His mother had sewn some gemstones in the hem of her coat, and they sold those to survive. His father finally got a hospital orderly job in Chicago because he couldn't get recognized as a physician in the U.S. They had left servants and a big house in Erfurt, on the edge of the Black Forest, for an apartment in an old tenement building in Chicago. When he was a master's student at the University of Chicago, his father died of a heart attack and his mother was committed for insanity.

They had both died of broken hearts. By this time, Doc's professors had recognized his abilities and made sure he finished his master's degree. He wanted to leave all the cold and hardships of Chicago so when one of his former professors was appointed to a Chair at UCLA, he contacted him. Dr. Weaver was one of the few highly respected black Psychiatrists in the field and Doc had been one of his favorite students. He made sure that he was in his program. While civil rights still had a long way to go, Dr. Weaver had never let that hold him back. He had gone to med school in the south, while staying with his grandparents. They taught him how to overcome racial obstacles with his wits.

Doc would come by and take Hope for a walk on the beach or a hike up a rocky road in the hills above Kona or a sail in a small catamaran that he had, so they could have time to talk. She liked that and he encouraged her to sing to him after he found out about her musical tendencies. Admittedly, she knew he was romancing her, but she ignored that part and kept it on a friend basis. He was old fashioned in that way and didn't push it.

When she told him about the trip to the Volcano, he said that he wished he could come with her, but he had to go to Honolulu for a conference at the University of Hawaii that his friend and sponsor, Dr. Weaver, was having. Right now, she missed him.

Hope was thinking of Doc, as she left the beautiful Koa filled house and walked out into yard with Wick, who opened the door for her to get into a big older two-toned Suburban. She was impressed that he was being a gentleman and thanked him as she settled in. He grinned back at her as though she had made the most charming remark, he'd heard all day. He glanced at her as he started the vehicle and said, "We may have to take some alternate routes because the Pele's Hair is blocking some of the roads, like I told you, it's like the tiniest pieces of glass when it breaks up.

I'm going to take the lower road because I want to check on the turtles at the black sand beach. There are several rare, endangered sea turtles in Hawaii's waters, including the green sea turtle, hawksbill turtle, leatherback turtle, and loggerhead turtle. From Punalu'u Beach, you can see turtles swimming offshore and basking on the beach. It's a great place to watch marine life. Our best chance of seeing them on the beach is midday with them typically returning to the ocean around dusk. It's close to 11:00 am, we will get there at just the right time. I'm assuming you haven't seen the black sand beach yet.

I can't wait to show it to you. Can you believe that we're here together? What are the odds? It must be kismet because I had a secret crush on you from afar back in Jersey."

"That's hard to believe. I didn't even know you then. David and I only dated for a couple of semesters before he transferred to Syracuse. He never mentioned you to me. David majored in psychology. Did you take classes together?" Hope was uncomfortable.

He smiled and said, "Relax, I'm just getting nostalgic about my school days. These visits to the turtles always do that to me. I majored in Marine Biology. My father died in the middle of my second year and it was bad. He got drunk and killed himself. He was an Iroquois ironworker, better known as Skywalkers. Iroquois ironworkers, especially the Mohawks, are legendary for their dizzying work in erecting skyscrapers and steel bridges. Mohawk men have walked and worked on nearly all of New York City's towering buildings, including the Empire State Building, where my father's father fell and died during its construction.

Anyway, after he did himself in, my mother and I kind of spiraled down for a while, my grades suffered and the next thing I knew, I was in Vietnam working with Napalm for the military."

"Wow! You've been through a lot. It must be great living here in that beautiful house and getting to watch the rare turtles any time you want. How are you earning money?" Hope empathized because she was now genuinely interested in his story.

"Well, I'm exploring my options. Right now, I'm living off savings and Anno'," he chuckled as he pointed out the window. Hope could see ocean ahead and a ribbon of black outlining it. They turned off the main road, bumped down a dirt path and parked near a stand of trees. This area seemed really secluded with no other people around.

When Hope stepped out of the car, she closed her eyes, turned her head towards the beach and let her whole body absorb the raw sound of the Pacific Ocean and the awe-inspiring beauty of the black sand against the deep blue sea. She was lost in the moment and almost forgot about the somewhat disturbing presence of the man who had brought her to this timeless place of Mother Nature's Spirit. Hope felt gratitude towards him if anything. Watching the ocean, she shaded her eyes and breathed deep the refreshing sea air. There was no hint of volcanic sulfur in it. She looked around and saw that Wick had taken a blanket out of the car and was spreading it on the ground under a nearby tree.

"I don't see the turtles out yet. We may be a little early. They should be here soon, though. They usually emerge by late morning. Come, sit and we'll wait a little bit and watch them come ashore. Shouldn't be long," he said as Hope looked on skeptically.

Hope sat on the blanket and curled her legs under her. Wick sat down and lit a joint of Kona Gold. He took a puff and handed her the joint. Hope hesitated but took it and puffed a few times. When she tried to hand it back to him, he waved her off and stood up as if to get a better view of the beach. The pot seemed to ease Hope's anxiety. She relaxed, leaned on her elbows, put her head back, and listened to the waves. It was truly a beautiful, mythical spot. The black sand created an otherworldly quality to this beach's landscape. Wick walked over to the car and came back with two Primo beers. Hope shook her head no when he offered one to her. He quickly guzzled both as he sat down on the blanket a little too close to Hope for comfort.

He leaned toward Hope and said in a low growly voice, "Did you hear us last night? That was for you, I was thinking about you the whole time."

"I guess Annoa didn't know that!" Hope countered with alarm.

He laughed, "Well, she got her money's worth."

"I'm not flattered or interested in your fantasies! Where are those turtles?" She said and started to stand up. He grabbed her wrist and pulled her back down.

"Listen, I'm not trying to mess with your head. I was just teasing you," he looked up at the sky, then he started to speak in a sexy thick voice as though they were in an intimate setting, even though he was speaking about the natural things around us.

"It's amazingly clear today considering the volcano has been going off for weeks. You know what I like about eruptions? They create a blank canvas that gives way to a rainbow of life. Some people see them as a force of death and destruction that wreak havoc, but volcanoes have produced more than 80 per cent of the rock on the Earth's surface. They dredge up nutrients from the bowels of the planet, spreading them in rock and ash that eventually break down into fertile soil. The steps to release the nutrients come from the combined efforts of wind, water, and microbes. Together they transform the landscape from shades of grays to red and yellow soils that soon explode into life!"

He was propped on his elbow, lying on his side, and had pulled her down into the same position facing him. Hope observed him like she was watching a Cobra. He was weaving and bobbing in mood, deed, and conversation. She thought that she could see why his nickname was 'Quick Wick'. His mercurial mental swings were hypnotizing. She could see the danger in that. Perhaps Doc's talking to her about some of his studies on personality disorders or maybe her own intuition.   She knew that she was not in a safe space if she was with him. She felt very isolated and indeed she was because there was not another soul around.

She began to move very slowly to try to stand. Hope didn't know where she could run to or even really where she was. He put his hand lightly on her shoulder and she went limp onto her back. She was trapped and decided that she had to take the path of least resistance. 'Ohm Tao' was the symbol that Godwin had painted on the back of his car. She started repeating it in her head like a mantra. She was afraid of this guy. Would he hurt her? Could she forgive or keep an open heart   of love flowing if he victimized her? Hope started to hum a blues melody, almost a moan. He was leaning over her. She looked directly in his eyes with her mother's best "no fear" stare. He starred back as he put his hand up her dress and gently rubbed her thigh until he reached her panties. He pulled them off with urgency.

"I've had a crush on you since I first laid eyes on you. Do you believe in love at first sight? This may be what we have here." Hope was shaking her head no. There was a lump in her throat and before she could get out the word no, he was kissing her passionately while putting his finger inside of her vagina. She did not resist or respond.

He didn't have a belt on his jeans He had his pants down quickly and entered her. She felt it like a wound. Hope had always enjoyed sex with the limited number of partners she'd had.   This was not that and she knew it would be difficult for her to deal with it when it was over. Wick, on the other hand, seemed to think that they were making love.

He was almost cooing to her as he thrust back and forth, even asking her if she was there, as he came hard and laid on top of her with his face in her neck, exhaling hard stale beer breath. She wanted to push him off and run into the sea, but his weight captured her. His body heaviness was not fat, rather hard sinewy muscle. She found no comfort in his attempt to cuddle, only reversion, fear, and anger. He was grinning when he finally rolled over and let her up. Hope faked calm as she pulled on her panties and let his semen drain into them. She wouldn't give him the satisfaction of seeing her clean herself up. She would maintain whatever part of her dignity she could glean from this situation.

He finally stood up after watching her for a minute and pulled his jeans on. He wasn't wearing underwear or a belt. He shaded his eyes towards the shore and said, "Look the turtles were watching us! They're out now." They were the witnesses.

All Hope could think was that, at least, he would take her back to her friends, now that he'd gotten what he wanted and saw his turtles. He hadn't hit her or damaged her physically. He had taken something that she had not wanted to give, though. They both knew that much. He had manipulated a situation so he could satisfy his lust, as simple as that. He could coo his bull about love at first sight and so forth. She was not buying what he was trying to sell to justify his sexual aggression towards her. She felt used not loved or made love to. The word RAPE jumped into her head. She rejected it. She had not fought with him, nor had he been violent, but had effectively snake charmed her. Hope just wanted to get away from him, off the volcano, back to the Kona coast and friends.

Chapter 11

Chiefs of the Trinity

Repast

Tears were blurring my vision by the time I crested Hayfork Summit, so I pulled over at the lookout to compose my thoughts and have a moment of Selah. I turned off the engine and listened to the wind blowing gently through the large, colorful Madrones.

Suddenly, two fully grown young mountain lions came out of the bushes. Their healthy tan coats were glistening gold in the sunlight. I sat very still, hoping no other cars would come by so I could watch them as they frolicked with each other in the clearing. They rough housed for a bit with each other then faded back into thick brush, when they heard a truck coming over the summit. Rare animal sightings were always a sign for me to pay attention. I sat for a little while longer and meditated on the musings of Hawaii that I'd just had driving up the Summit. The blues tune that I'd been humming when I was lured to and trapped at the black sand beach came back to me. I dug my harmonica out of my purse and began softly playing, *Keys to the Highway**. This settled my spirit, and I was able to drive the rest of way home to Dubakella Mountain with a peaceful mind.

My formal Fire Chief's dress uniform was a second hand one that I'd inherited from another fire district, so I was relieved when Camilla contacted me to ask if I would sit with her during the memorial service. She said she really needed me there as a friend. I agreed. Joanie said she would get their son, Kyle, who was a fire fighter too, to sit with her and Carpenter. Kyle wasn't just a firefighter. He was actually a strike-force smokejumper with the U. S. Forest Service. Smokejumpers are specially trained wildland firefighters who provide an initial attack response on remote forest fires. They are inserted at the site of the fire by parachute, thus the name Smokejumpers. In addition to performing the initial attack on wildfires, they provide leadership for extended attacks on wildland fires. I told Head Chief of the change in seating plans requested by Camilla. He thought it was a great idea. He said it would kill two birds with one stone because he would officially assign me the role of the Family Liaison Officer and it would show the community that Carpenter had family support from his son, a well-respected, elite Smokejumper. Jesse said that would keep tongues from wagging so much and give Carpenter a runway for saving face considering some of the harsh criticism he could still be facing. Kyle was so well thought of that it was good to remind the other firefighters of the contributions that Carpenter's family, including Joanie, had made to the profession.

Firefighter funerals and memorial services are ripe with tradition. These traditions are designed to give the proper respect upon the passing of a local hero who has put his or her life at risk for the public. Fire department customs play an important role in honoring firefighters who have passed. Although individual fire departments tend to have their own ways of doing things, there are many points of agreement on how to properly memorialize a fallen firefighter. The Family Liaison Officer discusses with the family the various options for a traditional funeral. There would be no body because Dixon had already been cremated after the autopsy had been preformed and certified. This meant that there would be fire fighting gear posed including a helmet and high bright yellow boots turned backwards. The color guards will be standing at attention on each side of the display. The casket flag is already folded properly on the display when the body has been cremated. Each officer and firefighter in uniform approaches the display, stops, says a short prayer, puts on their hat, comes to attention with a sharp salute, slowly lowers the salute, turns and returns to the assemblage. After the speeches, which will only be Jesse and Joe, the minister will say a few remarks give the benediction and then the three-bell toll will close it out. I had already discussed her wishes with Camilla. She was onboard with everything Head Chief had put on the agenda so I felt some relief that the service would go smoothly and to her satisfaction.

Since the Repast was going to be held at the Trinity Alps Golf Resort, Pete decided to attend that part of the memorial event. He and Momma played the 9-hole course first. She didn't play, but she enjoyed driving the cart and hanging out with him. The food was consistently good at the golf course. This was going to be buffet style so it would be plentiful. The memorial service went smoothly as I had anticipated.

Bagpipes played as a greeting for everyone arriving at Trinity Alps A blessing was said and Camilla thanked all of us for participating in the memorial service for her brother. Everyone at the Repast expressed the feeling that Dixon had been sent off right. Since not that many people attending knew the man personally or professionally, the chance to celebrate was more animated than it normally would be for a fallen colleague.

Graham Michaels pulled me aside and said all the legal matters were handled. Jesse came over when he saw us talking and thanked me for handling the family side of things.

"Head Chief, I kind of feel dishonest not telling her everything that's going on," I decided I may as well get it off my chest while I had both of their ears.

Graham chimed in, "There is very little she can do about it now. I guess she could file a legal claim or lawsuit. It is highly unlikely that it would get past a judge."

Jesse looked pensive, "If you were to tell her, is this a good day to talk about it?"

"She asked me to stay with her this evening and help close out the house and I've agreed to do it. If you don't object, I may broach the subject if the opportunity arises."

"Perhaps, I will come by tomorrow morning to see if she has any questions for me. Graham keep your calendar open because we may need you as well. We have kept our promise and put her brother away with honor. If she wants to open this can of worms, it won't be pretty," he had that Sam Elliott look in his eye.

I wanted to assuage him from coming on hard this, so I said, "She has money so that would definitely not be a motivating factor. Let me talk to her. It's hard to feel one is being duplicitous, especially with someone who considers you a friend."

"Okay, I'll go easy. I'm still coming by there tomorrow and I want Graham to keep his satellite phone available in case we need him to explain the legal ramifications."

My mother had already asked the restaurant staff to fix to-go containers for "the family". Folks were starting to thin out as I caught Camilla's eye and she looked weary. Head Chief and Pete took some of the packed-up food out to our vehicles, as the Repast seemed to be limping to a close. Camilla was riding with me, so I hugged my mother and Pete goodbye. Jesse said to Camilla that he would be over to check up on her in the morning and we all went our separate ways.

"I have a horrible headache," Camilla complained as she leaned back in the truck.

"We have about a 30-minute drive to Lewiston so why don't you close your eyes and rest until we get there," I glanced at her, and she looked a little shaky and ashen.

We rode in silence all the way to the little house on 1st Avenue in Lewiston that her brother had rented and where I'd picked her up before the memorial service. She had been waiting on the little sitting porch earlier. I had not entered the house then, so I had no idea what sleeping arrangements she had for me. I would get through the evening, even if the conditions weren't ideal. I carried everything up on the porch while Camilla opened the door and started taking things into house. She seemed a little better now that she'd had a little quiet time since we left the Repast. I was still concerned about her. When I walked into the house, I was not shocked that boxes were stacked up all along the walls. Other than a few large boxes, the place looked orderly to me.

"Believe it or not this little place has three bedrooms. I'm pretty much camping out in the spare bedroom where my brother had his office, so I have you in the back bedroom. I have been sorting through all these research papers that he had on the history of this area and a lot of maps, too. These big boxes here have all the digging equipment that he had. I put them in these big sturdy boxes to get them out of the way," Camilla seemed befuddled or making a point. I wasn't sure which it was, but I could tell she was feeling some kind of way. I knew she was no fool, so I felt that I had to say something.

"'Milla, let's talk story," I said using her nickname and a Hawaiian colloquialism.

"Okay, but first put your things in the bedroom while I get us something to sip on. Then come into the office so I can show you some of what he had here," she responded.

My mother always says that I 'can't hold water', meaning I'm not good at secret keeping, so I knew that I would fail to hold back most of what I knew of the situation from Camilla. I took a deep steadying breath and walked down the little hallway into the first bedroom being used as an office/bedroom. Piles of neatly stacked documents were on the desk, quite a few books in order on the floor, a couple of chairs, two floor lamps and a daybed jammed into the small space. I sat next to Camilla at the desk, and she pulled out a couple of small maps and laid them out on the desk. She laid a large magnifying glass on them.

"Our grandfather had family stories, but some seemed fanciful to me and our grandmother, too. My brother, on the other hand, was totally fascinated by the tales and took much of what Granddad Dixon said as gospel. Dad would just laugh and say that his father was an old fool. To keep his feelings from getting hurt, he learned to stop talking about the family myths with Dad or anyone other than Granddad. Dad had quite a bit of bitterness towards his father. That story is a whole other chapter that I don't want to get into right now because it involved my mother and has very little to do with this situation." She bent down, picked up a rather large light grey book and opened it to a bookmarked page. "Anyway, history books say that our great, great, great, grandfather, who was the Sheriff, slaughtered a whole bunch of people; all over one dead miner who had hit a producing mining claim. While they found his riderless horse and then his body. They never found any of the gold from the claim. This goes back a long way."

"Yes, I know the story and that's what I want to talk to you about. My family has a connection to the incident, as well. My great, great grandfather, Mule Skinner, was in the area at one point in time and he was involved with one of the survivors, who offered him the lost gold for his help. He refused it as blood money. This is really weird.   That's what happens when we start digging around in our shared history. This is what your brother was doing out there on that fire, digging around in shared history. He was not certified to be on the fire nor was he assigned to be there from his Fire Chief or the Incident Commander. No one knew he was there until, one of the water tank drivers came across his body. The lost gold bags were found near him. The driver panicked and took off from the scene because he thought he would be accused of harming your brother for the gold. You've read the autopsy report. You know he died from natural causes. There is no way he would have been certified if Head Chief knew he had stents. He was in the classroom training stage though, so his physical condition had not come up. Look, I'm not going to lie to you, this was a valuable recovery.

Jesse is coming in the morning. He will go over all the details with you. The Fire Chiefs Association has laid claim to the find and taken legal measures to secure it. I'm not sure myself exactly the value. I know it's big and the only place it could have been discovered, based on where the body was found, is near the Natural Bridge, which is now part of the Shasta –Trinity National

Forest," I concluded feeling a weight lift off my consciousness.

"Wow! That's a lot. I will wait to learn more from Jesse Whyte. This may finally put a hidden past to bed for our family," she looked relieved to know the truth.

"'Milla, I'm sorry I didn't tell you everything right away. I had some loyalty and obligation to the Head Chief and the Fire Chiefs Association. I was the main person assigned to investigate the incident because the guy that discovered the body was from my unit. He and his family have been in the business of fighting wild land fires for at least a couple of generations that I know of. I had to be fair to them and make sure he was okay, and his reputation wasn't ruined in all this. It wouldn't be fair for them to be collateral damage in this bizarre and unusual situation. I had to follow every protocol from Head Chief and the advice from the attorney. However, I told them both at the service today that if you and I discussed it, I was going to be straight with you,"

"Hope, mahalo nui loa. I'm exhausted so let's get some rest and discuss it with Jesse tomorrow when he comes. He can also put some of these boxes of tools on his truck and take them to the Army Surplus store in town, which is probably where they came from in the first place." We hugged goodnight and I retired to the back bedroom.

The next morning over coffee, Camilla seemed very pensive. She said to me, "You know, my grandmother always said that my grandfather was wrong about the gold. She said Sheriff Dixon had chased after the Wintu because they were stealing that old guy's cattle, the lost of which affected the food supply, as well as, the economy. She said there was never any gold involved. As a girl, I thought she made sense and was the practical one in the family. I admired her, but my brother was sold on Granddad's story. As usual, it was about the money. All those murdered folks have haunted and caused division in this family for generations and over gold!" Silent tears rolled down her face.

"I'm so sorry, 'Milla!" I didn't hug her because she was really withdrawn into herself, I could tell by her body language that she needed to process this whole thing.

I heard a vehicle pull up into the driveway. It was Jesse Whyte. I went out on the porch to meet him and give an assessment of the situation. He just shook his head, took a deep breath, and walked into the house. I poured him a cup of coffee and we sat down after Camilla acknowledged him.

She looked at us both for a moment and said, "Thank you, Hope, for being straight with me about my brother and Head Chief for giving him an honorable send off, despite the circumstances of his demise. This quest of my brother's that was passed down from generation to generation has caused friction in this family for ages. I know I speak for my son when I say, neither of us want anything to do with a monetary recovery for this treasure. Like your ancestor, Hope, we consider it blood money. Even if my husband had not left a sizable estate for us, I hold, that it would be important to the family karma not to profit from harm done to the native people and the whole community in this quest for that gold. However, I would like to know what will happen now and how will the treasure be used. What is the plan?"

Jesse went through the plan to benefit the community with her. Camilla agreed that it was an impressive plan and would give our somewhat impoverished rural area a shot in the arm. She asked if she needed to sign anything. Head Chief checked with Attorney Michaels who said he had everything done that we needed. We spent the rest of the day helping her pack up the items in the house and loading up Jesse's truck with boxes. He made a couple of trips to Weaverville to Army Surplus and came back with cash that he turned over to Camilla. In between, his comings and goings, we got to catch up some more on the goings on in our lives and mutual acquaintances.

"Did you know Brah-la's cousin, Annoa? It was her husband, who some say, killed Brah-la in this brawl, but no one was ever arrested. They said Wick, that's his name, had protection from Nappy Pulawa and the Hawaiian Syndicate. I know he had a reputation as a mean, backstabbing S.O.B. Brah-la was barely gone before he was putting Jackie and her little girl, Angel, out of the Puako house," she was rattling on about another situation in Puako.

I didn't hear anything else she said after that. My mine became a blank. I finally told her that I was going to take quick nap before Jesse got back because I was feeling a little spent with all the packing. She seemed to understand. I made my escape to the back room. By the time, I laid across the bed, I could barely catch my breath, as I was transported back to my earliest days in Hawaii.

Chapter 12

A Mighty Long Way

Eruption

Hope didn't say another word once they were in the car. Wick was chatting endlessly, although she could not discern one word he said. When the Volcano House came into view, she realized that she was holding her breathe. She got out of the car, inhaled, and rushed into the lobby where she headed straight for the bathroom. After cleaning herself off as much as possible, she slowly walked into the lounge. There was some kind of excitement going on that confused her. Deana hugged her and Godwin was acting like she'd suddenly become a star. Hope asked Annoa for a drink of water which she sipped slowly trying to pull her nerves together.

"Okay, what are you guys carrying on so about?" Hope asked in befuddlement.

Deana said, "Doc called Ted and said he was bringing a couple of big-time record producers back with him from Honolulu to hear him play. He told Ted that you should sing a few songs, too. Doc says they are looking for new talent. Apparently, he knows these guys from his days in Hollywood when he was married to one of the famous actresses. We need to get back to Kona as soon as possible."

"That's fine with me. When will the car be fixed?" Hope said looking at Brah-la. He shrugged and mumbled something like by'n' by. He was looking at her strangely.

"Who are these guys that Doc has lined up and when are they coming here?" Wick interjected stridently.

"Ted said that they'll be here this weekend He wants Hope to come to the house for a rehearsal session. We really need to get back to Kona right away. Oh Hope, we know one of the guys. It's Carter, Egg and Roadie's friend from school. Evidently, he's at Capitol Records now and they are scouting Hawaii" Deana said excitedly.

"Okay, I'll take you all back to Kona and Brah-la can bring your car when it's fixed. Brah-la call Nappy and let him know what's going down." Hope thought Wick started acting like he was her manager or something. Who was Nappy anyway and what business was it of his what was happening? Hope couldn't find the voice to ask questions.

The thought of spending another day or two around Wick was paralyzing and frightening for her. She saw Brah-la looking at her closely and she tried to hide the fear that was showing on her face. She went into her GRITS mode, fanning and saying this is far out.

Girls Raised In The South can always fake poise with a well placed "bless your heart" or "far out", as the situation required. Hope thought this bitterly because Wick was really giving her cause for concern. All she could do was try to never be caught alone with him again. He was not a trustworthy man and Hope was thinking that Brah-la knew it too.

Wick was behind the bar, talking to Anno'a and Brah-la quietly asked Hope if she was alright. She could only shrug and say she thought so, but time would tell.

Wick picked up a backpack at their house and they were back in Kona in record time. He was a speedster on the straight roads. They went to their place so Hope and Deana could freshen up. Then headed straight for Ted's after that, to discuss the goings on. Ted was working on the equipment and the guys started helping.

Hope and Deana got all the details from Viv, who really handled the business for the band anyhow. Evidently, other folks had heard from Ted or via the 'coconut wireless', that music producers were coming to town. On an island, where nearly everyone creates music, dances, sings, or plays an instrument, this was welcome and potentially exciting news.

"Apparently, Doc was at the University of Hawaii's Manoa campus for some conference he attended. These guys were there, talking to the University's music department about collaboration. Doc heard about it and turned out he knew one of them, Bob Clarke, from his days in L.A. when he was married to the actress. They both went to school at UCLA. Doc was telling him about the music scene in Kona and he decided to come over. I guess his friend or colleague decided to come too. The more they talked, the other guy, John Carter, realized he knew Hope, through mutual friends," Viv delivered all of this astonishing news in her dry British accent and laid-back manner.

"Why is everyone so turned up? Surely, you've had other music producers come here looking at all the talent on the island?" Hope opined nervously.

Viv shrugged and said, "Truthfully, a lot of music production had died down here for the last few years. The quality of the recordings has been poor because of the cost of equipment upgrades. Then there is The Company, the Hawaiian Syndicate. Those crooks want to dip their hands into or have control of everything, including entertainment production and the unions. Nappy's organization extorts a tribute from anyone wanting to do business in Hawaii."

Hope's eyes nearly popped out of her head when she heard Viv say that name. She put it all together that Wick was working for this guy who was a local big time criminal.

"What a bummer!" Deana exclaimed. "That must be hard on the professional entertainers who are trying to earn a living working at the clubs and resorts. I assume that Ted is a musician's union member, and this criminal element has affected him too."

"Yes, and I hope Doc realizes that he is stepping into some potential land mines because they have folks all over the islands spying and working for them," Viv cut her eyes towards the studio. Hope knew she was talking about Wick who could be heard running his mouth from the front porch where they were seated. "It's too bad word got out before they arrived. It means a bad element will be there and not for the music. Rumor is that they control a vast crime organization which has inserted itself in many aspects of the island life, not just the entertainment field, but the fishing industry, organized labor, as well as, Hawaiian cultural and rights groups. They will resort to extreme violence if necessary. Rumor is they have connections with east coast Mafia."

"If they are dealing with east coast Mafia, it must be from New Jersey. I know because I went to school there and it permeates the culture. I don't know that I want to sing or be involved with this now. It sounds like I could be biting off more than I'm willing to take on. Frankly, this is frightening when I really think about it," Hope said, as she thought about Wick's keen interest in the event and the fact that he was from New Jersey.

Of what Hope had seen of his temperament, it would be hard for him not to have some connections like that in his home community. Hell, even she knew a few. Some kids that she'd gone to high school with, in Newark, had parents or 'uncles' who were openly 'mobbed up'. One of the Italian guys at her high school had tried to date her. It had been disastrous for them partly because his grease-ball of a father was prejudice as all get out. Also, because the guy, who went by his last name, Tasco, was not very bright nor garnered that much interest for her mentally. He was handsome, well-built and an okay guy until he got around some of his goombah friends then he started acting like them. Wick has some of those same characteristics, Hope thought; except he was wily, cunning and had perfected charming public manners. She believed that was clearly a deadly combination and he was a dangerous man.

Members of Ted's band started to arrive and tune up for the rehearsal session. Glen, the horn player, was the other black guy in the band, besides Ted who played bass guitar. Glen, a little standoffish before, was now acting very nice towards Hope. Viv had said that everyone was crediting Hope with attracting the record producers' attention. This surprised the heck out Hope because she only knew Carter through her good friends in San Francisco. The rehearsal went well, and Hope was glad to take her mind off the awful encounter with Wick, even though he was lurking about. Everyone seemed to be ignoring him or skirting around him like a snake was in the room. Hope was thinking that these musicians probably knew he worked for that 'Nappy' guy.

On the way back to their house, Wick was flattering Hope about her singing and saying how the show would be great. No one else could get a word in edgewise. As soon as they walked into the door, Hope immediately told everyone that she was exhausted, said goodnight and went upstairs to her attic bedroom. The house seemed to quiet down after awhile and she fell into fitful sleep so that she didn't hear Wick creep into her room.

The next thing she knew he was in her bed with his hands all over her. Hope was afraid to scream so once again she just went limp and let him have his way with her. He tried to tell her that he loved her. Hope's quiet sobs finally drove him out of her bedroom.

She was really depressed the next day. He was all over the house with his strident laughter. The other guys, Godwin, Grady, and Tab were acting like he was entertaining. They were all sitting at the dining table talking story with him. Hope tried to slip quietly into the kitchen to get her morning tea. Before she could get out, he came in and pressed her against the wall. Hope once again went limp. Deana came into the kitchen, and he pushed himself off of her. She grabbed her teacup and fled the room to Deana's astonished, accusatory stare. Hope was sipping her tea and trying to calm herself when Deana tapped lightly on her flimsy bedroom door and came in.

"You know he and Annoa are serious. She's his old lady," she looked sternly at Hope as if she were a whoring bitch. "Who's next, Godwin? Now that you think you're a big deal or that you're going to be famous, you can take any guy that you want?"

Hope was shocked. She had never heard Deana speak to anyone with that kind of malice in her voice. She was almost always soft spoken even when something went down that upset her, like the time some guys we all knew came into the restaurant she was managing and paid with 'Digger money', after running up a high bill. This was so uncharacteristic that they both started to cry. Hope could not understand where this was coming from until, they controlled their tears and Deana started to explain.

She said, "We heard you and Wick last night! Godwin said if he had known you were up for grabs, he would have snatched you!" Hope was shocked because she didn't think that she had made any noise during the episode with Wick. Now she realized that he had.

"Deana, I'd never do anything to hurt you! I adore Godwin, but I would never sleep with him voluntarily. This thing with Wick was not voluntary. I truly don't want to have anything more to do with him. He keeps coming on strong to me," Hope pled.

This seemed to soothe Deana, they hugged, and she left with some modicum of her usual peaceful vibe. Hope sat there awhile thinking how Wick was a malevolent person who was careless with other people's feelings and didn't seem to care how destructively his actions affected others. She thought perhaps it was his being in the horrible war in Vietnam and coming straight back into society without some kind of re-entry protocols.

Maybe she was just making excuses for him. However, when she thought about what he told her of his father's suicide, immediately after that being sent into a bloody war, then his mother's death while he was so far from home; Hope almost felt empathy for him.

Although Hawaii was a spectacularly beautiful environment, he didn't have any family here, only friends and most of those seemed to be Annoa's. It was probably her fault for not acknowledging her intuitive wariness of him or she was just making an excuse for his bad behavior, she ruminated. Doc had discussed something with her about emotional problems of veterans coming back from 'Nam. She hadn't understood it all at the time of the conversation, but she was feeling it in a visceral way now. Hope had attended rallies in San Francisco demonstrating against the Vietnam War because she thought it was a destructive, politically immoral aggression with a high loss of life and limb. She'd written poems against it that were published by the Diggers and attended guerilla street theatre actions that the San Francisco Mime Troupe had put on. Since these encounters with Wick, she suddenly felt personally touched by the war. She heard a tap at her door.

Viv stuck her head in, "Good morning, Ted is downstairs talking to the guys. They called about the car being driven over soon. He asked me to see if you will ride with us to Akamai Barnes for the performance. He wants the band there earlier than usual."

She stared at Hope, who was nodding agreement, for a long moment, then asked, "Are you alright, dearie? You look tired. Get some rest, I'm going to tell everyone here to leave you be, so you are ready for the gig. Have you decided which songs you'll do? Never mind that, whichever ones you do, it'll be great. Rest your voice and spirit."

Viv quietly closed the door and Hope let the silent tears roll down her face because the kindness was so unexpected and needed. She decided to take Viv's advice, stay in her room and rest. She had already decided on at least a couple of the blues songs that she would sing: *Walking Blues** and *Keys to the Highway**. She wanted to do some traveling songs because she felt trapped in this situation with Wick.

From there, she would leave it to Ted as to what he wanted her to sing. They'd rehearsed several songs and genres, so she felt prepared in that way. Even though, right now, she felt emotionally fragile, making music usually soothed her. She laid across the bed and hummed to herself for a while before she fell into a deep slumber. Hope dreamt of her upcoming birthday in just a few days, right after the Summer Solstice. In the dream, she saw herself basking in a radiant glow of well-being and self-love. When she woke, she looked out her open window, which gave her a scenic view of the magnificent Kona coast and she saw the most beautiful sunset anyone could imagine. She felt that celestial influences harmoniously were aligning to support and nurture her through this transformational journey that she knew she was about to embark upon. One thing that she knew was that she was no longer afraid of Wick or anyone else. She also remembered some of the words that Empath had spoken to her at the Volcano just a few days ago:

'This is a very significant journey for you. It will affect your destiny path for the rest of your life. Do not allow anyone to destroy the Divine Gift of a wonderful spirit.'

Hope felt hurt and even violated by Wick. She decided that she would consciously focus on being in a better place and trust her angels. She didn't want this to destroy her.

She started singing an old hymnal from deep within, "You can't hurry God. You just have to wait. You have to trust Him and give Him time. No matter how long it takes. He's a God that you can't hurry. He'll be there, don't worry. You know, He may not come when you want Him, but He's right on time." *

Hope felt at peace whether things were as she had wanted them to be or not.

Chapter 13

Chiefs of the Trinity

Elders

Jesse came back for one last load to the dump, and I got out of the bed feeling better. While I was resting, Camilla had been busy, and the place really looked packed up. Jesse said his goodbyes and that if she needed anything he was available and to just let him know. He left to take the last load to the dump. Camilla said she had packed her brother's ashes and was taking them back to Hawaii for the traditional ceremony, when her son was able to be home in the islands and in attendance. Hawaii has its own version of a burial at sea when scattering the ashes of loved ones. Family and friends will paddle out on surfboards and canoes before proceeding with the service. Once at the ocean burial spot, they place the ashes, along with leis and flowers, in the water.

Since I have a touch of aqua phobia, in all the years that I lived in Hawaii, I never participated in one of these ceremonies. The most common cause of aqua phobia is a negative experience in water, like a shipwreck or a bad swimming lesson or a near-drowning. Learning to swim is a rite of passage for many children, but the process can commonly bring up latent ancestral fears and frightening experiences. My trigger was a near-drowning while on a family outing with my uncle and male cousins. Anyway, I told Camilla that I thought that was a lovely plan, even though, personally, I would not want my ashes scattered that way. I was not going to go into it with her. She probably didn't remember that I seldom got in the water during our Beach Mum days and then only if it was a really low tide and calm day. I never said why to any of the moms so there would be no reason for her to remember that about me. I wondered if her brother's mountain man spirit would be happy being cast into the ocean brink.

" 'Milla, do think your brother was a mountain man or a seaside one?" I broached.

"Oh, he really loved the mountains and truly felt at home up here in these hills. My grandmother and I used to tease him that he carried the strong spirit of our ancestral matriarch, who was part Kiowa. After all of the slaughter of the Wintu that he did, Will Dixon procreated with a native woman. If you look closely, you can see her in my face and skin color. Evidently, he brought her west from Missouri with him, pretending she was his slave. She died soon after they arrived here and he had a close family friend raise the child, while he paid for the expenses. Apparently, the child looked more white than native, so he was able to get away with it and elected Sheriff," she mused.

"As a mountain person myself, I'd like to suggest that you put him to rest right here in Trinity where your family goes so far back and has such a deep connection to these mountains. You can still do a water ceremony if you want because there are certainly many places along the Trinity River that we could release his ashes," I said.

"Traditionally, only the southern Wintu cremated their dead, but nomadic tribes like the Kiowa did. The Trinity River is the perfect place to get his ashes back to nature. The clear, burbling waters running from here at Lewiston to the river's North Fork are especially picturesque with its beautiful evergreen forests, mountainous terrain, wildlife, and incredible scenery, I don't have to tell you. This is where you spent much of your childhood. If your son agrees and can make it here that would be great. If not, I know that the Fire Chiefs Association would support something like this. Unless you want it to be more private, then I would be glad to support you," I said as I watched the idea take shape in her expression. She seemed to want to do what was best here.

"You know, I like it. This would be full circle and put this saga to bed once and for all. Ronnie was not particularly close to his uncle, so I think this is a good idea."

"I have a friend who is a Nor-Rel-Muk medicine woman. She might be willing to perform a ceremony for you. Your direct lineage to the massacre of her people might be problematic. I am willing to reach out to her if you want me to. A ceremony by a Wintu would be appropriate and cleansing. Her name is Buffalo Woman. She is a very spiritual, mystical person. She will understand the whole picture," I told 'Milla.

She was thoughtfully nodding in agreement while I was speaking and said, "When do you think she could do it? Can you talk to her soon? Should I ask myself?"

"Let me ask her and we will go from there. It's early enough for me to head home. I will stop by her place on my way through Hayfork and discuss it with her. You good here on your own until I get back?" I was a little worried about leaving her alone.

"I'm fine. I just need some rest. Glad that I got everything packed up and cleared out, though. Now let's just make the final step and I will feel good about going home."

I could see the weariness in her face and hear it in her voice. This had been quite a shock and journey for Camilla. Family karma was hard to deal with especially on your own.

I drove straight back to Hayfork so I could stop at Buffalo Woman's store to see if she was there and available to talk to me. The Dairy Farm Store was always busy, but she was a very giving lady and folks often just stopped to talk with her about their issues in the community. The Dairy Farm Store was an unpainted wooden building that had the comfortable atmosphere of an old country store. It had a covered patio on the side that had a few tables and benches on the covered entryway porch, where people sat eating homemade ice cream or sipping hot coffee and greeting other customers for a little gossip. The food inside was mostly self-service hot food with a twist, instead of hot dogs, they had falafel sandwiches and other healthier foods. I didn't see a spot and was about to turn into the swimming pool park across the street when Casey's big shiny truck on monster wheels started up its engine and loud music blared playing Garth Brooks', *Friends in Low Places**, that got my attention, so I waited for her to pull out and got a spot right in front.

Molly was at the register with a couple people in line. She gave me her megawatt smile and I mouthed, "Buffalo Woman?"

She pointed to the office in the back, and I went down the narrow hall to the small, cramped room and tapped on the door. Buffalo Woman looked up from her books that she still did by hand. She was a handsome woman sporting a mane of thick curly almost frizzy brown hair with a little grey mixed that hung to her waist and parted in the middle.

"Chief Hope! Come on in." she said in her deep voice and waved towards a chair.

"You look tired. I heard there was service yesterday for that fireman that died on scene."

"Actually, that's what I came by to discuss with you. His sister was my neighbor when I lived in Hawaii years ago. He was her half-brother, same father, different mothers.

Anyway, she thought of taking his ashes back to Hawaii for a scattering ceremony, but he was really a child of these mountains and didn't live there very long so we thought it may be a good idea to scatter the ashes here. You've probably heard that he is a descendant of the infamous Sheriff Will Dixon," I explained haltingly, although I knew she had the 411.

She held up her hand for me to stop, "My people lived in these mountains many generations. We fished the rivers for Chinook and hunted everything here from the rabbit to deer to the bear, but buffalo was not here. Do you know why they call me Buffalo

Woman, even though, I'm a Nor-Rel-Muk Wintun and we never hunted the buffalo?"

I shook my head no and she continued with a serious tone and look on her face, "One of my ancestors was a Buffalo Soldier. My great grandmother said when I was born that I had his wild wiry hair. He was part black and part Cherokee Nation."

Well, 'I liked to fell through the floor', as my cousin, Deacon Jr. G, often says. How many part-black, part-Cherokee Buffalo Soldiers could have wandered in this remote mountain area? Was this woman a long-lost descendant of Mule Skinner? Was the Universe throwing me another curveball in this whole situation? I was stunned into silence and just starred dumbly at my friend that I had felt a great affinity with since first meeting her when I moved here. She starred back with a twinkle of humor in her eye.

"So, I say yes, to wrapping up this long karmic cycle. I will perform the Death Chant at his scattering ceremony, for this will heal some and put many ghosts to rest."

Then she gave into a throaty laugh and said in her teasing voice, "Cousin, we have much to be thankful for because the Universe has brought us together to help the ills of our land. Of course, we have been here before and I am not surprised that we are here again."

Now, I have heard Buffalo Woman speak in mystical terms before but this was so personal. I felt that I understood what she was saying. I stood up, so did she and we wrapped our arms around each other for a long moment. I was still too shocked to speak. I nodded my head, mouthed a thank you and stumbled out of her office.

I almost forgot the half gallon of homemade vanilla ice cream that I always get when I come to the Dairy Farm Store. Molly had packed it for me already. She held up the freezer bag, so I dug in my wallet and paid the lovely lady with the mega smile.

When I got home, Chez greeted me like I had been gone a month. She ran down the long driveway barking and keeping pace with my slow roll. When I parked, she had her big paws on the door so that I couldn't get out until I waved the freezer bag at her. She recognized it as the ice cream that she loved. Momma and Pete were sitting at the table on the back deck to take advantage of the shade that time of day so they could see up the driveway. They were watching and laughing until I got closer, and they saw my face. They sobered up and started asking me what happened. I held up a finger that signaled I would be right back as I went into the house. I washed my hands and scoped up bowls of ice cream including Chez' special ice cream bowl. I set ours on a tray and hers' on the side porch because she was standing there looking into sliding glass doors.

When I brought the tray out, Momma and Pete had a look of concern on their faces. We savored the delicious ice cream for a moment before I finally said to them, "Something extraordinary has been revealed! I went to talk to Buffalo Woman about doing a ceremony for Mr. Dixon. She is a Nor-Rel-Muk, and they never hunted buffalo. The biggest game they hunted was bear and deer. In fact, their main food staple was Chinook salmon. So why is she called Buffalo Woman? As it turns out, her great grandmother called her that when she was born, and it stuck. She called her that because she had an ancestor who was a Buffalo Soldier that was part black and part Cherokee!

Buffalo Woman was born with his mane of wiry hair. Momma, how many people fitting that description do you think lived in these remote mountains during those days? Do you think she could be a descendant of Mule Skinner? She was aware of our family story as it relates to this area, but she had never said anything until today. When I asked her about participating in the Dixon's scattering ceremony, she agreed because she basically said that we are cousins and must help heal this land as she believes we have done in the past. She is a mystic and in so many ways a mystery that I am inclined to believe with her."

My mother starred at me thoughtfully then asked, "How old is this woman?"

"About ten or twelve years older than Hope, I'd guess," Pete correctly observed.

"Well, GG Skinner used to say that he probably had a 'squaw' or two in some of the places where he'd done his 'walkabouts'. No surprise there because he was gone for months sometimes. Then during his Buffalo Soldier stint, it was years. He always came back to her though and in his latter days, he stayed home and worked on getting Hardy Grove Church built. When can I meet our newfound Cuz?" Momma laughed ironically.

"I was so stunned that I didn't even try to firm up arrangements for the ceremony so I will have to see her again anyway. We can go into town tomorrow for breakfast at Irene's and stop in at the Dairy Farm Store. She's usually there most of the day," I said.

After we finished our ice cream, I went upstairs to my office to do some research on the Wintun historic tradition. My satellite was slow, but it worked well if I was patient. I called Camilla to let her know that Buffalo Woman had agreed to perform the native ceremony called the Death Chant. She was excited and we discussed the best location, date, and other details that I had researched. I still needed to run it by Buffalo Woman to make sure that we were in step with the tradition. I told Camilla that I would let her know later the next day when I had things firmed. In the meantime, she should decide who she wanted to invite to the ceremony because I expected it to be quite a big deal locally considering the family histories. I told her about the revelation that Buffalo Woman had given me. I asked her to keep it confidential because it was still kind of raw and not really confirmed. I mentioned that my mother was going to meet with Buffalo Woman for what she called a 'powwow'. Camilla, who had met my mother for the second time at her brother' Fireman's Repast, reminded me that she knew how formidable 'Alley Cat' could be, because she'd met her in Puako when my child was just a baby. She had me cracking up reminding me of the battles between Momma and Doc that I had shared with the Beach Mums. We hung up with an exchange that we hoped Buffalo Woman would still agree to the ceremony after the 'powwow'.

Breakfast at Irene's was eventful, but satisfying once Momma got the cook straightened out about what she expected from a menu that said, "fresh everything".

The cook shouted, "OK, OK, you make it sound like we're going to poison the whole town!" He was laughing at the same time because Momma was really humorous.

Pete drove next door to the post office and package pick up store, while Momma and I walked up to the Swim Park parking lot and across the street to the Dairy Farm Store. Oddly enough, Buffalo Woman was sitting out front on the bench by the door, as if she was expecting us. She stood when we got to the porch and spread her hands towards the covered patio like a maître d. We went up the two little stairs and sat at a table with a small bucket of iced water bottles. We were the only ones on the patio, as if she had closed it for a private party. Buffalo Woman put a chain across the opening.

She sat down and reached her open hands out on the table. We each took her hands and sat in silence for a minute or two. She looked deeply at Momma and said, "Welcome, my sisters. For now, we know we share Sawal Mem, Sawal Suhana; Sacred Water, Sacred Life, for our ancestors have mingled. I am a direct descendant from Lol-chet Pok'-ta, the Old Woman, the Shaman who died at the Natural Bridge Massacre.

Family rumor has it that a mule man helped her great grandson return for vengeance on some of the raiders. Then they both disappeared and never returned to these mountains. Now we have a chance to put this bad blood away and go forward towards a higher plane. That is why I agreed to do the Death Chant even though it is very difficult duty for me."

Momma was so moved that she couldn't speak, just nodded in affirmation. I decided to get down to business and asked her if the time that Camilla had chosen was good. She agreed to it but suggested a change in location. We finalized our plans, hugged, and all agreed that this felt like the right thing to do.

Momma was subdued as we got into Pete's van which was parked right in front. He'd gone into store while we were talking and gotten some more homemade ice cream because he knew we'd want something to share later when the three of us got a chance to talk it over. As soon as we got to Joyland, which is what we called our place, I went to my office to call Camilla. I knew she was waiting all morning to hear, and it was already almost 2:00 o'clock. She picked up immediately and I told her about the meeting with Buffalo Woman, but that she wanted to change the location to the Natural Bridge where Hayfork Creek was running full. The early morning time chosen was just after dawn when it would be light enough to approach the location, but too early for tourists that came to what was now part of the Shasta-Trinity National Forest. We planned to meet across from the Dairy Farm Store at the Swim Park parking lot. Jesse was going to bring Camilla so it would just be a few of us. Camilla was pretty worn out and wanted to get back to her quiet beach life in Puako. I told her that I understood the strain on her.

When Pete, Momma and I arrived at the park early the next morning, Buffalo Woman was already there sitting on a bench in the back of Casey's big pickup truck. She was wearing the fanciest long deer skin beaded tasseled dress that I've ever seen and had a crown of bear claws sitting in her lap. Casey was behind the wheel. As soon as we pulled in, I saw Jesse's truck turning in next to us and waved to him and Camilla. The Nor- Rel-Muk Community office was a few doors down from the Dairy Farm Store. Even though it was early, several old Wintun men were standing out in front by the road. I recognized a couple of them, George Walking Bear and Herman Wind Catcher, tribal elders.

Jesse got out of his truck, walked over, inclined his head towards them and said, "Is there going to be trouble?" Buffalo Woman shook her head no.

He got back in his truck. Jesse and I were born on the same day so I knew he could be combative, but this was not the time nor the place. We slowly caravanned past them as they chanted low and mournful with hats in hand; then on through the unusually light early morning town traffic out towards the turn off. The Natural Bridge is located off Wildwood Road, which is a high and winding connector between two main thoroughfares for these tiny towns and remotely located ranches and cabins, Highway 3, and Highway 36. Buffalo Woman rode on the back of Casey's big truck, like a Queen Goddess with her hair flowing behind her in the wind. She did not put on her crown of bear claws. As we rose higher in elevation on Wildwood Road, a mist seemed to rise up from the forest floor or maybe from Hayfork Creek, I'm not sure where it was coming from, but it created a hushed shroud over everything.

When we arrived at the Natural Bridge, there were several folks on horseback and a few vehicles as well. I had not invited anyone so I assumed that the word had gotten around town through the rumor mill. I recognized the town librarian/historian and her father. I saw my neighbor, Blackstone, who always wore her hair in two long braids and kept several horses. She was on her favorite, a huge horse named Princess. A few people in town who were actually from Hawaii were there. This included the electrician's wife and her cousin, who was married to a retired Sheriff plus Greg, Molly's boyfriend, a strikingly handsome young man, who seemed to adore her.

Hawaiians revere the ancient traditions of honoring ancestors, and they practice hanai, which is a term used in that culture to refer to finding your tribe or being adopted in. Doc used to say that I was hanai when he would refer to me as "Lili". I was not surprised that there would be some folks that would be interested in this situation. Joanie and Carpenter were there, as was Attorney Graham Michaels. Casey's mother and father were also there on horseback.

A few others I did not know, but I had seen around the county. Momma was looking around in wonderment and leaned over to ask in a hushed tone, "Who are all of these people?" Pete, a preacher's son, answered before I did.

"A great cloud of witnesses," [1] he said in his preacher father's voice, as we left the van.

Buffalo Woman put on her crown of claws and the bench was placed on the ground as a stepping stool. She was helped from the truck by the four old tribal elders, who had arrived right behind us. Camilla stood close to Jesse, clutching the container with her brother's ashes. She looked terrified so I went over and wrapped my arm around her waist. I felt her relax a little, but tears were already flowing down her face as we all walked to the center of the Natural Bridge. It is not only a historic site, but a geologic wonder, a high rock arch of 150 feet long and about 30 feet high. As we slowly hiked up the limestone arch over the flowing Hayfork Creek, the area felt spectacular and mystical.

Buffalo Woman stood in the middle of the bridge with all of us arrayed on each side of her. Time seemed to stand still, and a strange silence filled the air. Then Buffalo Woman lifted her crowned head, roared like thunder as she began the Death Chant with, "Ollalbis! Ollalbis! Awaken the spirits of the dead! Raise the legions of fallen warriors! Protect your people! The Wintu are gone now. There are few of us left. As time passes only the spirit place will remain. Those of the white blood will come to this place many times to see where we died. One man came to this place to seek answers. He is no more. His blood is of our brother's blood from the land to the rising sun. We all lived the lives and felt the death. He is forgiven. Ancient Ones receive your child!"

She emptied the container into the stream. From deep within her bosom came a deep moan that sounded like more than one person as the crescendo of her wail increased.

She started to sway and move from side to side. She began an ecstatic trance dance. Her soul and spirit seemed to leave her body as the tribal elders held her up to keep her from falling over, as the earth quaking moans subsided into a low unintelligible chant We had picked rose petals from my garden containers so as the tribal elders helped the Shaman down off the arch, I handed out handfuls of rose petals for the people to toss into the creek after the ashes.

We were all spent and carefully made our way off the bridge. The elders took Buffalo Woman to their vehicle, and they drove away without another word. Molly's boyfriend said that they were hosting a coffee breakout on the outdoor patio at the Dairy Farm Store for all of us to come on by for fellowship. Most of us were drained, but none of us could turn down Molly so we all nodded and the folks on horseback left with a promise to stop by. The Fairgrounds was just up the street so they could all put their horses in the fenced quarters there. We were all exhausted from this very emotional ceremony and the shared experience, but we didn't want to be apart. Even Pete and Momma were willing to go.

I decided to ride with Camilla and Jesse, even though it was a tight fit in the truck, because I was concerned about Camilla's state of mind. She took my hand and held on tightly. She looked at me intently and then said, "I'm going home tomorrow. I must get back to my beach. Hope, why did you move here? It is such a strange place to find you. Help me understand the dynamics?"

Her question took me back to the process that this unusual journey was for us.

Chapter 14

Out Lands: Living Off The Grid

Hanai

Sitting in my skyscraper windowed office, looking at downtown Sacramento, my eyes blur and I see my forested hillside land in the Trinity mountains. I sketch out the log cabin that I want to build there, then I get down to the brass tacks of how do I afford to even clear a spot to put in the well. This month, we're going to buy a heavy-duty chain saw. That is all the budget can handle – a chain saw. How in the world are we going to get up the cash for the five-thousand-dollar well? That's an estimate. To be as sure as possible, we've hired a Well Witcher and come Spring, he'll tell us where to dig and how deep. My husband is skeptical, but he doesn't want to pay for a dry hole so he's going along with the idea.

My motivational inspiration back in tack, I get down to my job of selling ads into the four magazines that I am responsible for producing. We will use my quarterly sales commission checks to pay cash for the improvements on our mountain property.

All the groundwork will be in place before we start on the cabin. Out of necessity, we plan for a totally self-sufficient place. The community is so far out that there is a real lack of public services, including electricity, communal water source, garbage pickup, sewer, or postal delivery, even though there are about seven hundred people there. Of course, the population often drops dramatically during the snowy winters.

In the early spring, we head for the mountains to meet the Water

Witcher, who turns out to be quite a scientist. I have to admit that we expected some mumbo jumbo type of thing. To our surprise, his "divining rods" are actually a specialty metal, and he uses several other kinds of measuring devices to calculate the best well location. The process is so fascinating that my husband, a mathematician who has worked at IBM for over twenty years, is captivated and spends the whole morning amusing himself by playing with the Well Witcher's instruments and taking loads of pictures of the whole procedure. The Well Witcher also has satellite maps that show the underground watercourses. It turns out the maps are available to anyone through the County Resource Conservation office. He finally marks the recommended placement for the well drillers and gives us a pretty tight estimate of how deep we can expect to dig before reaching an excellent water source.

After much conversation with the well drillers and partial deposit, we have a drill date for the summer to coincide with my next quarterly commission check. We are excited and curious to know if the $500 we spent on the Well Witcher will be worth it. The driller says that they often recommend that the customer use a Witcher and the one that we selected has an excellent reputation. The Witcher came highly recommended from a local neighbor.

As the summer date gets closer, I anxiously watch my receivables to make sure that there will be enough money to pay the well drillers and the pump installers. It must be enough over in case the well goes deeper than predicted by the Witcher. I get lucky when one large advertising client pays immediately to secure a premier spot on one of my annual magazines. It bumps me to the next tier in my compensation package and I breathe easier knowing I can order the top of the line well pump.

I'm so excited that as soon as the snow melted, I talk Pete into a "quick" trip up to the mountains. We take sleeping bags and sleep in his new van. We freeze our butts off and I decide that we need a camper up on the property, especially while we're rebuilding. Pete agrees that we will need a construction office. We want to pay cash for everything including the log cabin so we both think that the idea of a 'construction trailer' is just a way to stave off the obvious, that we may never actually build. However, we plan anyway. Pete sniffs out contractor names from fishermen when he's at the lake; at the local hardware store; and friendly waitresses at the town's one main restaurant. He collects the names and brings them to me with whatever information that he has about them, like a cat bringing presents of dead mice. He's not sure what I'm going to do with it, but he's proud of his kill. Pete really wants me to believe that he has faith that we can get this done, although I know that he is quite skeptical. In the meantime, every chance that I get I'm searching through design books, reading up on solar energy and penciling costs.

During one of my research frenzies, I read in one of my back-to- the-land magazines about harvesting trees and using them to build. I know that I don't want to do this because we want Cedar logs, and we have no Cedar trees of any size on our land. But it does give me an idea of how I can finance my septic tank. I get Pete to take a brief fishing trip up to the mountains and ask around town about a small logger that might be willing to work with us. I was too busy at work to go. Pete didn't mind a quick roughing it trip without me. In fact, I think he preferred it. As it turned out, private lot logging was about the only kind going on in that part of the mountains because of the Spotted Owl in the area being put on the endangered species list. Large plot commercial logging was difficult and expensive to get permitted. Since this area was considered Spotted Owl country, many of the smaller loggers didn't have much work.

We began a big learning curve on what it meant to own, log, and sell commercial timber in an endangered species area. First, we interviewed loggers because we wanted someone who select logs and leaves the land neat by cleaning up the tree slash; clean up some large, rotted logs that we had laying around; widen and rock our long driveway; put in a septic system; and do it all for the money that he collected from the logs. A few years back, we might have been laughed out of town but, now as it turned out, Pete discovered several willing guys with logging operations.

We chose an operation run by two families, Hale & Kane. Pete started jokingly calling them Raising Hell & Cain. He'd call me at work and say I wonder if they're Raising Hell or Cain today. It was actually funny the first ten times he said it, after that I told him, don't you accidentally call them that to their faces. Of course, the very next time he saw them, that is exactly what he did, but they thought it was funny too.

I explained to Camilla that this land came to me at a real crisis point in my life. My grandfather, who was my solid rock when I was growing up, died just when we got back from Micronesia. My marriage to Doc was rocky and we were going through transitioning back to the states. We didn't even have a house at the time, and we were living at the Silversword Inn in Kula on Maui. Our house in Puako was leased out. Doc arranged my travel back to the east coast for the funeral, but when I got to L.A. I found out that he had messed up my connections and I would not make it there in time for the funeral. After several hours in the L.A. airport, I ended up turning around and coming back to Maui infuriated, frustrated and heartbroken that I would not be with my family during this time of grieving my beloved 'Papa'.

A few of months later, I found out that he had left Heir land up here that he had inherited from his grandfather. During the crisis of a broken relationship, this land became my touchstone, as if my grandfather and his grandfather were looking out for me. I used to come visit the land every vacation and commune with nature here.

When Pete and I got married, I told him that I wanted to stop in San Francisco on our way to Hawaii for our honeymoon and drive up to the land where I wanted us to retire. He fell in love with the picturesque area, the idea of living remotely and fishing the pristine lakes close by and living off the grid. He took an early retirement offer from IBM. We sold the Florida house, packed up, and headed for the closest real city to the land, which was Sacramento, where I had accepted a position.

We spent the next five years, working to attain our dream of developing my "legacy" land and building a log cabin on it. We had planned on living here part time, but once we built it and got to know the community, we decided that this would work for full time. We both started working from home on various consulting contracts. It worked it out pretty much as we had envisioned.

I knew this explained how we got here, but that was not what Camilla was really asking. Her question was spiritual. What guided us here was what she really wanted to know. That would take a much longer and deeper conversation than the time in the truck, so I had just given her the bare outline of the why and the how before we arrived at the Dairy Farm Store. In my opinion, she really knew the answer because, considering her family karma, we had a shared experience. She was most likely feeling unsure of herself or her understanding of the way the Universe works or manifests itself in our lives because Buffalo Woman's ceremony had opened all our hearts, or as the eastern mystics say, Chakras, to a highly spiritual and kind of unexplainable portal. Camilla had never seemed like a shallow person to me, so I was certain that she understood my role and purpose in her life at this point in time.

The conversation put me in mind of another one that we had long ago at Puako Beach when the night before many of us heard heavy footsteps sounding as though they were on our roofs. The Beach Mums speculated that it had to be Night Marchers, death dealing ghosts, known as Iuaka'i po in the Hawaiian language. Folklore describes them as groups of spirits, sometimes traveling with ancient Hawaiian gods and goddesses in their midst that march down the mountainside to the beach at night. These ghostly entities are said to have traveled through places called Night Marcher trails. The area of Puako Beach was considered one of the trails.

Some of the Beach Mums were really spooked, but 'Milla and Jackie took it in stride and expressed little worry, but said it was part of the Hawaiian way of "na'u", which means "mine". They both said since no one was harmed that indicated that one of the warriors or Night Marchers had recognized us as a descendant or/ and a Hanai (adopted into the family), so the procession passed us by without causing harm. Since they were both married to Island guys, this settled the nerves of all of us other Beach Mums and we had a pleasant day with our kids. I mentioned that to her, as we walked arm in arm onto the Dairy Farm Store patio and she nodded in understanding.

Gregorian, Molly's boyfriend, was already there setting up a small stage area and getting out instruments. I didn't know he was a musician. Since he was from Hawaii, I should have guessed as much. I was really surprised when he unpacked a 12-string steel guitar, which was my instrument of choice. Then he blew us away when he started playing it and singing an old Gabby Pahinui song. The two ladies from Maui immediately started dancing the beautiful, graceful ancient style hula. 'Milla visibly relaxed and enjoyed the beautiful traditional song, *Ipo Lei Manu**.

Gabby Pahinui was a master of the steel guitar and the best slack key player ever. This great musician was a driving force in the reawakening of interest in Hawaiian music, also in all things culturally Hawaiian. Gabby played a very important part in the rise of what became known as the Hawaiian Cultural Renaissance. Music recorded by him in the 60's and 70's was enormously popular and influential, especially his group, Sons of Hawaii. This beautiful soul died at the early age of 59, a month after I left Hawaii and moved back to the mainland. The man was a true legend in music and culture. This song took me back to my early days in Hawaii when I first heard this melody, as it was being performed by Gabby himself, a truly amazing artist.

Chapter 15

A Mighty Long Way

Flash

The dramatic sky of the setting sun made Hope realize that she was hungry She went downstairs to the front yard and picked a large ripe avocado butter pear. With a little sea salt, it was a perfect meal for her. She also enjoyed eating a small, sweet papaya for breakfast and she picked one off the little tree near Godwin's studio.

She headed back upstairs to her room where she had a knife and a sea salt grinder because she didn't want to go into the dining room or kitchen where Wick was hanging out, running his mouth. However, just as she got to her bedroom doorway, which opened to the outside, Brah-la drove into the driveway with the repaired car. He saw her and tooted his horn, waving and grinning like he was happy to see her. She waved back, mimicking his enthusiasm because she genuinely liked him. She sat her harvest on the table and went back downstairs to greet him.

He got out of the car and beamed at her, "Bum car all fixed! Hey, you ready for tomorrow? Gon' be a big day! I found out my hanai cousin, Gabby Pahinui coming over to Kona. Man, this brudah can sing and play da kine slack key! You never heard such soulful playing. Just wait, you see!"

His enthusiasm was palatable; so much so, that Hope affectionately draped her arm around his waist and they walked into the main house, chatting away about Gabby and his music. Wick and several other folks were sitting at the big Koa table in front of the screen-less picture window with a couple of punks burning to ward off mosquitoes. They were drinking Primo, smoking 'pakalolo' and eating 'pupus' that Deana had sat out for the wonderful ritual of Kona sunset observation that everyone did almost nightly. Hope and Brah-la walked in just as the famed mystical purple flash happened and everyone oohed and ahhed, when the blazing red sun sunk into the truly blue waters of the Pacific; briefly, they became one and turned purple.

When he realized we'd walked in arm and arm, Wick nastily slurred at Brah-la, "Wha' you so happy 'bout, Brah? Car fixed? Did you handle the business with Nappy?"

He talked to Brah-la like he was his servant. Hope glared at Wick, just turned, and left. She went to her room and enjoyed eating her perfectly ripened, large butter avocado. It was becoming intolerable having Wick around. Hope was determined not to let him spoil her good vibe, so she stripped down to her underwear, laid across the bed, cleared her mind and did some deep breathing yoga while humming quietly to herself. She relaxed under the cool breeze from the window and dropped off into a deep sleep.

Hope was not sure how long she'd slept, when the smell of beer breath woke her, and she knew Wick was on her bed. He was not touching her, just lying there staring at her. When he saw that she was awake, he immediately rolled over on her, pressing his weight so that she could not move and telling her that he loved her. Hope struggled to get control. He was pulling down her panties before she could get him off her. She realized that he'd already taken off his jeans. She went limp when he entered her, but something inside of her rebelled against this invasion of her body. She clasped her legs around his waist and with all of her strength she rolled him until she was on top. She rode him hard and forcefully until he came, screaming her name. Hope collapsed on top of him, then she rolled to sit up. He tried to pull her back down on him. Hope saw and snatched the large paring knife, that she'd used to cut the avocado, off the bedside table. When she rolled back on him, she had it at his throat.

She said with fierceness, "If you ever touch me again, I will kill you graveyard dead. Do you hear me?"

He tried to laugh, but he saw her eyes and pushed her off him, grabbed his jeans from the floor and as he slipped them on, he said in a derisive, but shaky voice, "Woman, you're no killer. You're a healer besides I just put a baby in you, so you'll be tied to me forever! See you around, Mama!" He slammed the door behind him.

Hope was stunned and sat there for a couple of hours until dawn broke then she went downstairs and took an outdoor shower. She stood under the water for a long time.

Deana was moving around the yard, gathering fruit for breakfast. Hope eased back up the stairs because she didn't want to encounter anyone. She spent the entire morning in her room in a state of near panic remembering what Wick said because she could not shake the disconcerting feeling that it was true. She did not want a child with this man. She certainly did not want to be tied to him 'forever' as he had stated. Hope felt odd about it because she had climaxed along with him, even though it was really her body not her mind reacting to the stimulation. She always got her period around her birthday, so she knew she was probably ovulating. He could possibly be right that he'd impregnated her. Of course, abortion was illegal. She didn't have any connections in Hawaii for a "back alley" operation. Abortion was the kind of thing that was kept hush- hush among women everywhere. Most men didn't know who did them. Most women wanted it that way.

Hope shook herself out of this depressive revelry and picked up her notebook with her poems and songs. She refused to let herself get down over something that may or may not have happened. The main thing was that she had gotten Wick off her back, and she intended to keep him at bay. She spent the rest of the morning writing.

The healing effect of that creative activity steadied her nerves. She worked on her hair, makeup, and outfit for the evening performance. By the time Viv came by to get her, she was "feed, puffed and powdered", as her Momma would say, and ready to go to Akamai Barnes.

Brah-la rode with Viv and Hope into Kailua so he could help Ted with the equipment. He was always helpful to other people and Hope liked that about his spirit.

Doc and Carter were already there with some other folks. They both greeted Hope with hugs and introductions. Doc was acting like a doting parent as he took Hope's hand and led her over to a table with a big ruggedly handsome kanaka and said with some pride, "Gabby, this is the lady we mentioned to you earlier," Hope shook his hand.

"What's your name young lady?" Gabby said with a hint of humor in his voice.

Hope answered, "Hope."
Doc interjected with, "Lili is her Hawaiian name."

Gabby laughed and said, "Yes, I see the resemblance. I hear you can sing. So, Lili Ho'olana are you ready to take your place in the line of Princess Liliuokalani?"

Hope was flabbergasted because she had read some of the Hawaiian history of the Ali'i. The hanai Princess Liliuokalani and last Queen was one of that era's most fascinating people. She looked into Gabby's ancient eyes and saw a whole line of the African Diaspora that she had never contemplated before. Hope was struck dumb by this ancient soul connection. Gabby nodded his head as if to acknowledge the feeling then let go of her hand and took a deep swig of his drink. Hope knew he was an 'old soul', as her great grandmother used to say, and she was honored to be in his presence.

Brah-la came to the table with a tall red-haired 'haole' girl by the hand and said, "Cuz, I want you to meet my girl, Jackie. Haole girl loves me. She'll marry me!"

Jackie blushed, leaned into him, and said, "Oh Howard, you're so dramatic!"

Everyone laughed because evidently no one called Brah-la by his given name, Howard.

Gabby said, "Well, I hope you are as happy as me and my Emily. We've been married since we were teenagers and many keikis later, we're still in love. She overlooks a lot of things, but I try to be the man she wants me to be. You try too 'Howard'."

Hope hugged Brah-la and Jackie, who gave her a warm happy smile. Hope sat back at the table with Doc. Jackie and Brah-la sat with them. There was some loud talking coming from the large booth in the corner where Wick had joined several guys. Jackie whispered something to Brah-la. Hope overheard it as "ignore them".

Wick staggered over to our table, kissed Jackie on the shoulder, slapped Brah-la on the back of the head and started to come towards Hope. Doc shook his head and put out his arm to block his way. He had caught Hope's tensing of her body when Wick came to the table. Wick drew back his arm like he was going to punch Doc, but Brah-la was out of his chair quickly and grabbed his arm. Hope had picked up a knife off the table because she wasn't going to put up with any more intrusions from this man. Jackie was up too and grabbed Hope by the arm and quickly took her into the ladies' room.

"How does Annoa stand that nasty guy? He thinks that he can do anything he wants and get away with it, doesn't he? She's a nice person. Why is she with him?!"

Hope really wanted to know what was happening there because she couldn't fathom spending her time with someone so abusive and disrespectful.

Jackie looked at her sadly, "He plays on Annoa's sympathies. Her father suffered from manic depression and eventually killed himself. Wick seems to have the same condition. One day he is up then the next time you see him, he's like he is today. His own father committed suicide so Annoa is afraid that he will too. She has actually found something to love about him!"

They heard a guitar tuning up and knew the music was getting started so they went back out and found a calmer scene with all the guys at their own tables, except Gabby who was on stage and about to perform. Hope thought he was going to do a solo, but she saw Ted on the base and someone she didn't know sit down with a zither. Hope got excited because she had a zither that she played. She'd left it in San Francisco.

As soon as Gabby hit the first note on his 12-string guitar, the whole atmosphere of the place changed. We were all transported away on his slack-key rhythms, melodic voice, and the beautiful Hawaiian language that he sung in. It was like a fresh breeze blowing through our heads. Hope loved both the 12-string guitar and the zither. This soothing, earthy sound was just what she needed. Brah-la leaned over and told her the name of the song was *Pu'uanahulu**. Hope really loved it. Tears flowed from her eyes. It was a release of emotion that she didn't expect. It felt good to let go of the tensions. He then played a song she had heard before and loved called *Ipo Lei Manu**.

Hope saw that Carter was really enjoying the music. He was as fascinated by the sound as she was. Hopefully, he would be able to facilitate a more widespread distribution of this wonderful music genre. Hope knew that he was an influential figure at Capitol Records and the music industry in Hollywood. She assumed that's how Carter actually knew Doc, from his days in Hollywood when he married a big name 'studio' star. Doc seemed to have fond, if not nostalgic, memories of those days. Hope wasn't sure why the marriage didn't last. It was Hollywood, sometimes glitz and glamour is not all it's cracked up to be. That was something that Hope learned in New York City. Real life hits you whether you are rich or famous or talented or none of those things. It was hard to hide from trauma.

She came out of her musings when Ted's full band joined them on stage. They did a couple more numbers with Gabby and took a break to thundering applause. Ted came over to their table with Gabby and told Hope that he wanted her to do the next set. Gabby told him to introduce her with her Hawaiian name, Lili Ho'olana. Ted was surprised, but Hope could tell that he was pleased. When the next set opened, Ted played one of his popular songs then gave Hope a grand introduction which made her a little nervous.

She sang her first song, *Keys to the Highway**, and it was well received so she felt bolder. The next number *You Don't Know What Love Is** went even better so she was soaring when the band unexpectedly led her into the next song, *You Can Have Him**, which she belted using some of her own adlib lyrics; then she took out her harmonica, morphed into *Walking Blues** and the band followed perfectly. She got a standing ovation as she bopped off the stage while playing her harmonica all the way back to her table. Hope waved off calls for one more number and pointed to her throat as if to say her voice was going. Truthfully the songs were just too emotionally overwhelming for her right now with Wick in the room. The band played one more number and then took another break.

Doc and Carter suddenly jumped up out of their chairs, blocking his access, just as Wick lunged at Hope. Clearly, he was drunk and yelling some kind of nonsense at her.

Gabby and Brah-la wrest him away from the table. Doc took Hope outside and asked if she wanted to leave. Hope could only nod that she did. He took her to his car and went back inside to tell Carter. When he came back, he told her that they were going to his house in Puako because he didn't think she should go anywhere that Wick could find her right now. She nodded numbly because this whole thing with Wick had really boiled over into a public display of animosity. His guilty conscience must have made him think that the songs that Hope sang were directed at him. Although he inspired them with his behavior, they were popular songs that Hope could relate to and gave her an insight into emotional situations. However, they had triggered his wrath. He seemed to be out of control and making threats towards Hope. He was also still angry over her putting a knife to his throat and telling him that she would kill him if he ever attempted to have sex with her again. Hope did not regret that move at all, but he was still stewing over it. He also seemed to have a drinking problem, like his father.

On the way to Puako, Doc was silent for a long time, then he asked tentatively, "What happened between you two? Didn't you just meet a few days ago?"

"He claims he knows me from our college days in New Jersey. I don't remember him at all," Hope sighed in deep melancholy. She didn't want to tell him about the unwanted sex, but it seemed inevitable, considering how emotionally charged the situation was with Wick. She took another deep breath and told Doc what happened at the volcano and then at the house. Hope decided that since Doc was a psychologist, he was a resource, in a way, that could help her deal with all the drama and trauma of it.

"You haven't told Deana what happened?" he asked shocked that I had not told.

"No details, she accused me of trying to steal Annoa's boyfriend and expressed that I might go after Godwin. She really hurt my feelings and we've been kind of not talking and avoiding each other since we got back from the volcano," Hope explained.

"That must have left you feeling very isolated," Doc empathized.

"It was good to see you and Carter. Even Brah-la has been very kind to me."

Hope felt relieved to tell someone what was going on and she fell into a deep sleep. When they arrived at Doc's house in Puako, she could hear the pounding surf, but it was dark, and she could not see the surroundings. Doc gave her a large T-shirt to sleep in and quietly closed the bedroom door behind him. Hope slept like a baby and didn't wake until the morning sun grazed her face with warmth. She sat up, stretched, and looked around the comfortable room with bamboo mats over polished concrete floors.

The bedroom had its own bath, so she went in and found toiletries left for her. Doc had also left a muumuu for her, so she had a change of clothes. She dressed in gratitude for his thoughtfulness. Doc could be a little crazy, but he was basically a good guy, if you caught him on one of his good days, Hope thought, chuckling to herself. She could hear the ocean even in the bathroom, so she wandered out following the sound towards the sea. Hope sat on the sandy rocks by the sea, meditated and a poem came to her that she had written on the beach in Kona, before she went to the volcano with Godwin and Deana.

She hummed to herself, threw her arms wide and recited the little poem word for word.

> "Sea Spirits that dance against
> The Sands of my Mind
> Show me there is no Time
> Only the Waters of One
> As foaming illusions subside
> Into the evolving Life Tide.
>
> While sitting by the Ocean's Door
> Wondering and wandering -
> more and more
> I watched the Sea for Signs of Me
> When on a wave I heard my name
> Ohm- from the drop of water came."

She called it The Rootless Root.[4] Hope was not sure why, but it seemed right at the time she wrote it. Sitting by this little rocky beach, across the road from this quiet oasis of Doc's just brought it to mind.

She slowly walked back to the house where the smell of Kona coffee tickled her nose and desire for a mug of the stuff. She never drank coffee until she came to Kona. The coffee that grows in the hillside rain forests of the Big Island is 100% pure Kona coffee, a rare commodity exclusively grown in north and south Kona. The high elevation, constant cloud coverage and rich volcanic soil in the upland slopes of Kona create an ideal environment for harvesting this unique Hawaiian coffee bean. Hope could taste the difference from the beverage served on the mainland.

Doc was bustling about the kitchen and had fruit, toast and coffee laid out for her. She sat and contentedly ate what he'd sat in front of her. She finished eating and he said, "I have something important to tell you. I hate to upset you. However, you should know. I received a call from Ted this morning. Late last night Wick and a couple the thugs that he was with at Akamai Barnes, came looking for you. They beat up Godwin and Tab. They will be alright. They ransacked the house and acted all kinds of crazy. Deana is unharmed. Godwin made her hide out while this was going on. Wick was evidently mainly looking for you. It's a good thing that you were here, or it may have gotten even worse according to Godwin. Ted has advised them to not get the police involved. I'm going to contact Lt. Abreu at the sheriff's office because we have worked together before when people were in crisis. Even though, Ted says that Wick has a lot of connected people to protect him, I'm going to ask Lt. Abreu to warn him away from you. With my position at the State Health Department, I can exert some influence."

Hope burst out crying, "Oh my God! Are the guys alright?! How bad were they hurt? Deana is probably beside herself with worry and anxiety. She is a true 'peace-nik'. What can I do to make this right? I feel like it's my fault that this all happened to them."

"You know better than that. They don't blame you. It is the mentality of some of these guys returning from this war theater. They have problems that are not being dealt with. They are visiting their emotional and physical ills on the communities where they live and the people they are interacting with. I'm working with Dr. Weaver, I forgot that you know Fred, on getting a study grant to develop data on this. These guys were exposed to a very powerful chemical in Agent Orange. I'm sure that it affected them."

"I'm sorry, but I can't handle the excuses for Wick right now. I'm worried about my friends. Are they safe from him and his thugs? I'm just sick to my stomach with this."

Hope suddenly felt the anxiety physically. She bolted from the table, ran to the bathroom, and threw up everything that she had just eaten. She felt drained of energy and stayed in the bathroom for a while applying a cold-water cloth to her face and neck.

When she came out, Doc sat her down in the spacious living room, took her hand and told her that Ted and Viv had taken everyone at the house up to his place in Honaunau. Doc said that he had 5 acres up in the hills above Honaunau Bay. It was hard to get to and not easily approachable, but a comfortable house once you got there. He said he didn't own it but had a 50-year lease from the Bishop Estate that he'd obtained as part of his position with the Health Department. He went on telling her that it was a safe place for them and in the tradition of ancient Hawaii. Honaunau means "Place of Refuge". The ancient Hawaiians fled there for safety or to seek absolution after breaking a kapu or law. Honaunau was the original seat of the Kona chiefdom and the ancestral home of King Kamehameha and the Kamehameha dynasty.

He held Hope's hand and talked to Hope in a calming voice until she stopped shivering and felt better. She settled into the comfortable couch and let the sound of the waves soothe her into a nap. She was startled awake by the ringing of the phone. She settled back again when she heard Doc greet Carter. Doc came out of the kitchen and said Carter called to say he was headed back to the mainland. He would get back with her on some ideas that he had for her singing career. Hope wondered when it turned into a 'career' because she was just having fun and enjoying making music.

She considered herself a writer and businesswoman. She probably should think about leaving this place of great beauty to head back to her business in the City. Hope's two associates were still taking care of things, but she didn't know how long they could cope without her. She still paid rent to her roommates at their shared apartment in the City. Carter had briefly said something to her about him and Egg getting together as a couple. Hope wondered if that meant Roadie would be trying to carry the place on her own.

She felt irresponsible, like she'd let her girlfriends down. Deana was on the run because of her. Roadie might end up having to take care of that big apartment alone. The place was nice and large. It was a rare find in Twin Peaks with a view of the city and the Bay. While she was here, she decided to make a few phone calls and get caught up on the scene in the city. She would pay Doc for the long-distance calls.

She was deep in thought when he came in and said that he had a concern about her, "You should see a doctor as soon as possible. You have been raped or at the very least sexually violated against your will. You need to see a gynecologist."

"You're right, I'll have to ask Viv, but I don't want her to know what happened. It is just too much to get anyone else involved in this mess," Hope reluctantly agreed.

"I have a guy in Honokaa that I know. He's a good doctor. Let me see if I can arrange an appointment with him if that is alright with you," Doc was in his role now.

Hope felt safe with him, especially when he had his 'medical professional hat' on, and she knew that he cared. She couldn't disagree with him that she needed to see a doctor. Things had moved so fast that she hadn't had time to think of the things she needed to do to take care of herself and get through what she realized was a life crisis. Hope felt lucky that she had an experienced friend like Doc to help deal with this thing. She decided to live in the moment and enjoy the sense of security she felt being with him.

Chapter 16

Out Lands: Living Off The Grid

Aloha

Molly shook me from my transported thoughts of Hawaii and asked me if I would join her and Greg on the mike. I dug out my trusty harmonica, not sure what they were going to jam, but I was up for it. Molly and I had talked about our love for music when she met my son whose name was Mele, Mel for short. She found out that he was born in Hawaii, so she was keen to introduce him to Gregorian, Greg as she called him. Whenever Mel came to visit, he liked to hang out with those two.

Probably because of my conversation with Camilla, I launched into *Gonna Move Up To The Country (Paint My Mailbox Blue) *. We then did a rousing version of the song *Going Up the Country* *and everyone joined in singing, except Momma, but she clapped along. It was a great ending for a momentous event for the community. We all appreciated the vibe of healing and love that had been created and hugged each other as we went our separate ways. Camilla and I said our goodbyes with a promise from me to come see her when I came to Hawaii again.

Pete had picked up ice cream before we left the Dairy Farm Store so when we got home, we changed into some comfortable clothes and sat out on the back deck with our bowls and Chez, to discuss the extraordinary day.

"Now that was the Aloha spirit that I experienced when I was in

Hawaii, and I loved it. How about you? Did you feel the same way? Did it feel like that to you, too?"

Pete asked Momma and me, as we nodded in agreement.

"Yes, that was an amazing ceremony and scattering repast!" I was enthused.

"You know, I haven't heard you sing since you were a child, other than in the church choirs and that wasn't solo.   This was very special to me. It was soulful blues," Momma said, looking at me with a touch of pride. Momma was the best at negative motivation, so this was high praise for her children to get approval from her.

Pete said in a teasing tone, "She can sing the blues to me all night long."

"Look out now! Don't make promises you can't keep. Anyway, I'm glad this part of the issue has successfully been put to rest. Now, we must make sure the funds are distributed without a lot of conflict when the money shows up," I mused. "We'll be getting together on that next week or the week after depending on the paperwork and other legalities. Momma, you'll be gone home to Florida before then. I know you'll want to know all the scoop. We'll keep you posted on the drama," I laughed.

"I've been gone from home almost two months. I was in Chi-town for a month helping Dorothea with that crazy man. It was actually a good thing that I was there for them. Then here, but it has been a lot of fun and, you know, I love traveling and seeing new things. This has been an interesting trip," Momma always referred to her former husband as "that crazy man" and he referred to her as "Woman Crazy". It was a running joke with the family because they had five children together, now adults.

We talked about family and relationships until late afternoon, then went around to the front deck where we could have a better view of the western sunset and it's reflecting off Dubakella Mountain. No one was hungry so after feeding Chez, I sat while Pete lit the fire pit and threw a few fragrant pinecones on it which kept bugs at bay. We sat outside enjoying the quiet evening with an occasional hoot from an owl.

Our area didn't have noisy nighttime cicadas because we were in Spotted Owl country, and they feasted on them. Most of our evenings were peacefully silent. Exceptions to that rule were the occasional screech of log trucks air braking over a mile away on hilly Highway 36 during logging season and rifle fire during deer hunting season.

Momma was asking me when I started singing the blues. I decided to give her a little history of my musical patchwork journey. Although she had visited me often, the closest we had lived to each other was 300 miles away. We had lived at least a 3,000-mile distance for most of my life. I went in and got my 12-string guitar. I told Momma about when Doc and I went to China. We spent some time in Hong Kong, and I bought the12-string there. Once we returned to Hawaii, I took private lessons and music classes at the University. I'd never actually played it for my mother, so I decided to give her a taste of my original music. Many of the songs that I have written were very personal and part of a healing process for me, so I had little inclination to sing in public anymore. Pete had heard some of my songs, but mostly I used them as a source of inner strengthening, as music is for many folks. The guitar was tuned and ready.

The first song I sang was called, *Easy To Love Man** and my mother really liked it because she picked up on the chorus and started singing the melody along with me, "Cause I'm your sister, mother, woman, lover and you're my good brother, friend and husband, easy to love man. I launched into another torch song called, *Bill Came Through**, after the second verse she caught the hook and sang that with me too.

"But never had nobody leave me till Bill, till Bill came through." Momma got my songs, and she pointed out the irony in the verses which we all laughed about it.

Pete sees irony as "God's Humor" so he said that's why he always enjoyed my songs.

We only had a few more days before my mother was leaving to return home to Florida.   We really treasured these moments of sharing with each other. We wanted to make it a celebratory few days. We decided to treat ourselves to a weekend at the Flying AA Ranch & Lodge overlooking the best fishing lake ever. Momma had not been to the lodge. She loved fishing so this would be a wonderful treat for her. The Flying AA is a working ranch and the lodge itself is "rustic", meaning bad beds, dated décor, but very clean with great food and a wonderfully picturesque setting, nestled between the mountains and the lake where it meets the river. It is a family-owned and run cattle and timber ranch with its own airstrip, so it gets a variety of outdoorsmen. In addition to the ranch hands, there are all kinds of folks that come for a stay. Depending on the season, there are the Pilot Clubs, deer hunters, bear hunters, bow archers, white water rafters, fly fishermen, trout, and bass boaters, RVers, hikers, mushroom hunters, rock climbers; everybody from yuppies to roughnecks.

The owners are on site and mostly family run the place.   The atmosphere is that of a very fun house party. They have a gigantic outdoor barbeque pit off the bar and a huge deck that the dining room opens onto next to the bar, that overlooks the river, airstrip, and swimming pool. Pete and I love to sit on the deck and spot planes as they float down off the Yolla Bolly mountain current into the river valley to gently touch down on the landing strip.

The chef is a cousin of the family, and he has been cooking there since he was a kid. He is the size of a large bull, but he makes the biscuits that taste as good as any southern black woman's. My Kansas City born and raised husband, who considers himself a barbeque aficionado, says this guy's grill skills are second to none. This chef will also clean and cook your fresh caught fish if you want him to do it. We do a lot of bragging about the guy's culinary prowess to entice Momma to want to go. It doesn't take much because she loves an adventure if there is a good meal promised at the end.

Pete makes the arrangements, hooks up his bass boat to his truck, loads up Chez, all before I can get my clothes on the next morning. Momma and Chez are both ready and excited to go. The Lodge allows pets and Chez knows what it means when the boat is hooked up. She is a Chesapeake Bay Retriever water dog and really loves swimming.

She is supposed to be a duck hunting dog too, but she doesn't like the sound of guns or birds in large flocks. Pete always teases me about her flunking out of dog training school. When people compliment Chez on what a fine-looking dog she is, he says, 'Yeah, that dog won't hunt', quoting from a Texas saying made famous by a well-known lady politician. Chez looks at him like she understands. You can almost hear her saying, 'Well, I haven't seen you hunt anything either. I'll hunt when you do.'

Flying AA Ranch normally takes about an hour to drive the winding roads, but towing the boat slows us down some. Highway 36 is a well-maintained road, but it has more S-curves and steep hilly climbs than most folks like. We always stop at the lookout peak along Highway 36 with a view of the entire Ruth valley area and the Yolla Bolly Wilderness, which means 'Snowy Peak' in Wintu. The view is breathtaking and worth the slight delay. North Yolla Bolly Mountain is a 7,868-foot peak in the Klamath Mountain range of the Coast Ranges located in Trinity County, California.

The mountain is in an isolated part of the Yolla Bolly - Middle Eel Wilderness, in the Shasta-Trinity National Forest. It is situated about 13 miles from Mount Linn (South Yolla Bolly), the highest point of the Coast Ranges south of the Trinity Alps. The mountain divides the headwaters of the South Fork Trinity River and Cottonwood Creek. A spur of the mountain, Skylight Ridge, touches the headwaters of the Middle Fork Eel River, making it the triple point between the Klamath, Sacramento, and Eel River systems, the three largest waterways of Northern California.

When our mothers visit, Pete and I like to hang out and do normal things with them. Then we always plan something special for their trip and this was Momma's for this time. She had never been to this part of the country, and it was a wonder-world landscape. The lake, which was really a dam, was breath catching. As we crested the hill that led down to the launching dock for the lake, I heard Momma gasp at the stunning scenery. I leaned over and told her that it was just as beautiful at night especially during a full moon as it was in the day with the pristine clear water. Pete told her that the fish out of the lake were firm and delicious. Pete launched the boat with a little backing up help from me and then loaded us all up for a day on the lake.

I let Chez dip in the cool water, then dried her off before she came aboard the bass boat. Chez immediately settled down with a contented grunt and we motored out to Pete's favorite fishing cove, where I pointed out an Osprey, that really looks like a bald eagle, perched in a nearby tree, waiting for Pete to attract the fish so it could swoop in and steal one or two from him. Chez's ears perked up when I pointed out the Osprey and she kept one eye open watching for the bird to see if it would come near. I opened a novel that I wanted to read and Pete fixed Momma a fishing pole so she could "wet a line" and we passed the morning in leisure with Pete pulling in a couple of nice size rainbow trout and a big, large-mouth bass. Momma got a smaller bass and screamed so loud the Osprey woke up and tried to swoop in. Chez was aggressively barking at it, and it veered away. Chez was not afraid of one bird even a big one, just didn't like them in flocks. Pete said the bass was too small to eat and tossed it back.

With the sun high in the sky and the day warming up, Pete said the fish had gone into hiding and we motored back to the Marina. He docked the boat for later since we were going to spend the weekend at the Lodge. We drove the rest of the way to the Flying AA Ranch, which was another twenty-five minutes although it was less than 15 miles away, the road was winding and slow going. It was a beautiful scenic ride, so we didn't mind. Pete checked us in, took our bags to the adjourning rooms and went to talk to the chef about fixing his catch for our dinner. It was Friday and I like to eat fish on Fridays, just to make sure that I intentionally incorporated it into our diets.

As the Assistant Fire Chief, Joanie was on call this weekend; and after handling the Dixon family events, I was glad to get the break. We often got busy during the weekend, with tourists coming out for outdoor activities, especially motorcyclists and ATVers. I didn't even bring my radio because it annoyed Pete when I carried it around when off duty. I tried to clear my mind of the worry that something might happen while I wasn't there. Joanie knew where we were. She would call the Lodge office if something happened because there were no phones in the room and only satellite phones worked on this side of Yolla Bolly mountain. One of the things that the Fire Chiefs wanted to use the gold proceeds for was to put up a communications tower near the summit so that this area of the County could communicate with the other side of the mountain better during an emergency. Joanie's son Kyle lived in this area at the U.S. Forest Ranger station in Ruth during the summer. He was another contact if needed. This eased my mind some too.

Momma and I changed into fresh tops and walked leisurely to the bar. Chez was tethered to the balcony where she could look out over the scenery, so she was fine. If we sat out on the deck off the dining room, she could see us. Also, she could smell the barbeque grill and anticipated that she would get a treat out of the deal. We had drinks, great grilled trout, and fried bass along with homemade hush puppies. Chez was happy with her barbeque and after a brief romp, went to sleep on the balcony in her portable carrier.

The day ended with live music including fiddles and a tub bass. I knew one of the fiddlers from my work at the County Grants office as the Affordable Housing and Grant Consultant when needed. His young, widowed daughter and her child had qualified for the land grant development program. Her husband had been killed in a car accident on the way home near the junction of Highways 3 and 36. Our fire department had been the first responders on the scene. Joanie and I were the ones to contact the Sheriff's station in Ruth about the accident so the widow could be notified.

This was not my favorite memory as a Fire Chief. It did give me satisfaction to know that I helped her in an important way to overcome a difficult life crisis. They had a piece of land that they wanted to build on. He was trying to earn the money required. He was working extra to make that happen. Tragically he got over tired and fell asleep at the wheel. As an aide at the local elementary school, she was able to qualify for the program and her father was instrumental in getting a builder, who hired him to build the log house right along the river. Her father had the experience and the skill, but not the contractor's license. Her land was in an ideal spot on the lake. I could sit on the deck at the lodge and see it across the river.

Anyway, we were friendly. He asked me to sing with the band. I said okay for just one number. I was really here to relax with my mother. He understood. We did *Country Roads* *. I added a few lyric changes that included our location, Yolla Bolly instead of 'West Virginia' and folks went wild for it.

When I sat down, Momma leaned over and asked, "How is it that we're the only black people for 100 miles around here and you know everybody? They know you and that you can sing and jam when I'm just finding out." I shrugged it off, nodded my head and gave her my 'we're winning' smirk. She burst out laughing. I knew my mother was having a good time which is what Pete and I really wanted for her.

We went out fishing with Pete the next morning early. After he caught his limit, we made it back to the Flying AA before they stopped serving lunch and had some of their great barbeque. We rested during the heat of the afternoon. When we went for drinks at the bar, there was talk of a wildfire near Wildwood, which was just on the other side of Yolla Bolly and only a few miles from Dubakella Mountain. The Pilot's Club that was there decided to pull out before visibility was badly affected. I contacted Joanie and she said we were on Forest Service standby because the fire was on their part of the mountain. Pete knew I couldn't stay here and relax with a wild land fire in my area of responsibility. He loaded the truck and Chez, picked up the boat from the marina and headed to Dubakella Mountain. When we got home, it was very smoky.

Momma said, "Well, it was fun while it lasted. I enjoyed. Thanks, you two. It looks like Hope is going to have to get to work. There's a fire that needs putting out!"

FLYING DOUBLE AA CA
FLY-IN RESORT

Chapter 17

Chiefs of the Trinity

Fire

Pete and Momma handled getting the truck, boat and dog unloaded while I went straight upstairs to my desk, called Joanie to let her know I was back home. Then I raised Head Chief Whyte on his radio. He said he was at the staging center. I asked if Joanie and I could come and get an in-person situation update and he agreed that it would be good for us to do that. Joanie picked me up in a Chief's utility truck and we went rattling over the Wildwood Pass, a curvy drop off ride of about 15 miles or half an hour in good visibility. The closer we got to the Wildwood Store, which was the staging area, the thicker the smoke became. The usually sleepy, log building that is the Wildwood Store was awash with frenetic activity. Some the folks looked surprised when I walked up, in my Chief's uniform and red hard hat, with Joanie. Most of them knew her because she had worked at the airport on the coast where the emergency helicopters and the air water tankers landed. She was considered an expert at directing landings in bad weather.

In the whole United States, less than 10 per cent of fire fighters are black, and more the shame, even fewer are Chiefs, especially in wildland fire units. Head Chief Whyte took us over to the Cal Fire Incident Commander and introduced us. Since we were the next fire district and community to the west, he took the time to give us an in-situ briefing. It seemed to dawn on him who I was. He said he remembered reading my Fire Mitigation Stewardship grant proposal, and really liked it. Head Chief Whyte interjected that we now had private sourced funding for our proposed program. Jesse winked at Joanie and me when he said it because we knew he was referring to our literal found pot of gold. The Commander was enthused by this news because one thing about California Department of Forestry and Fire Protection (CAL FIRE), they are dedicated to the fire prevention, fire protection, mitigation, and stewardship of the over 31 million acres of wildlands they oversee.

The Department provides varied emergency services in most of the State's 58 counties via contracts with local governments, so having a good relationship with them was essential to our local fire departments. Preventing wildfires in the State Responsibility Area is a vital part of CAL FIRE's mission. CAL FIRE adapted to the evolving destructive wildfires and succeeded in significantly increasing its efforts in fire prevention. They work with communities to prevent wildfire through wildland pre-fire engineering, vegetation management, fire planning, education, and some law enforcement. They systematically identify and help us with high priority fuel reduction projects and other measures to protect as many wildfire-vulnerable communities as possible. They are wonderful partners to local remote communities and fire departments like ours. I was on mission and my best, most charming behavior because, truthfully, we needed these guys to help us keep our homes and beautiful environment safe.

The Commander told us that about 3,000 acres were burning. Only about 10 per cent was under control at this time. He said the good news for us is that it was burning towards the tiny town of Platina to the southeast and not towards us to the northwest.

We took a walk around the layout with him. They had already set up the food truck and dining tents. The shower tents were in the parking lot and the laundry truck had arrived. They were moving the big dumpsters across the road to a large clearing. Dumpsters can draw bears even if they are bear proofed; hungry bears will try clawing the metal tops off.

We sat at one of the wooden picnic tables under the tents and the Incident Commander asked if Joanie might be available to help with air traffic control. He knew that with her experience she would have a good idea of where to direct the air tankers and smoke jumpers' helicopters. Joanie had her bag of gear in the truck, and I knew she always carried her folder with her certifications and licenses in it. She kept her creditials paperwork on point. She was ready to report for duty at any time. I looked at Joanie and I knew that she wanted to do it because if they brought in the smoke jumpers, her son Kyle's team would probably be involved. She would want to be on the scene to do any and everything she could to help him.

Head Chief knew that too, looked at me and said, "I can take Chief Hope back to Dubakella Mountain and you'll have the utility truck to drive back. We have some details to discuss anyway. Commander, you have everything you need for now if this burn stays under 20,000 acres, you have the manpower to handle it. If it gets beyond that, we'll call out the local reinforcements."

When Head Chief and I got back to my fire station, I kind of stuck out my chest because my team was busy at work. Even Carpenter was there, refilling the water tank and gassing it up. Santa Cruz was testing the communication devices. Blackstone was checking the hoses and equipment on the old engine.

We planned to order a new engine when we got our funding. I had all the paperwork done for a grant with Rural Development including a completed build out design from the engine manufacturer. We just needed the matching funds. The gold money would be the resource for that. I hoped that Head Chief had some news on the situation and that's what he wanted to discuss with me. We had only talked about fire operations driving over Wildwood Pass. I could tell that he had something weighty on his mind.

When he saw Carpenter, he said, "Good, Carpenter, just the man we need to see." Hope knew that she was right. He had some news about the disposition of the gold.

He waved Carpenter over and we went into the Fire Hall Community Room. Head Chief had a folder with him that he opened once the three of us were seated. He passed both of us a sheath of papers with a cover that read <u>Disposition of Funds – the Fire Chiefs Assoc</u>. "As you can see, we've worked out the details of the gold recovery dispensation. The gold weighed in at close to 200 pounds! It was a tremendous treasure which then converted to a little over $6,000,000 in today's market. Graham had quite a time keeping this find quiet. The fact that we are such a remote community has helped and Camilla's cooperation was a blessing, too. Hope, your friendship with her and the loving way the community supported her was a tremendous help. Each Stakeholder in this, including you, Carpenter, will receive $600,000. This will pay Attorney Michaels' fees, the Fire Chief Association as the Administrators, Carpenter's finder's reward, and all of the county's Fire Departments that have their qualifying financial paperwork up to date.

If we can agree on this soon, we can start the process of fund disbursement. In the info that I just handed you, is everything we need for you to sign to get this show on the road. How does that sound to you all? Any questions or comments?" Head Chief asked.

"Our department's latest financials and the audit are on file with the Association so we should be good. Is this considered a settlement for Carpenter? Will he have to pay taxes on this money?" I felt a need to stand in for Joanie because I knew she would be asking these types of questions and in a protect mode for Carpenter.

"Attorney Michaels has worked it all out and it's in his packet so he can take it home, read it or call Graham for an explanation. I don't pretend to understand all the legalese. He tried to set up everything to all our advantage and I think he succeeded."

We all knew Graham Michaels had as good of a legal mind as we could find, especially around these parts. Carpenter and I agreed that we would review the settlement and sign. I was certainly eager to order the new fire engine and equipment.

Carpenter wanted to talk to Joanie first. We knew it would be a few days before she was back home from the Wildwood fire even if it was controlled in the next few hours. He did say, however, that he agreed with the amount, especially, since it was an even split among all the parties. Receiving over a half million tax-free dollars should sound good to someone who was basically impoverished, I thought.

There was a tap on the door and Blackstone stuck her head in. She asked if she could show us something. She brought in a little Spotted Owl in a shallow box, wrapped in a hand towel. Her normal peaches-and-cream skin was red with frustration, So she said, "The guy from the Bay Area that just bought the log house on our road said he had field mice in his garage. In his ignorance, he used rat poison instead of traps and this little precious is who he found when he came home for the weekend. The owl must have eaten a field mouse who'd ingested some poison. What part of, 'we are an organic community', didn't he get, Morlan, when we went to introduce ourselves as his nearest neighbors?" Blackstone used her last name and called everyone else by theirs as well.

Before I could say anything, Head Chief Whyte jumped into action. He grabbed his radio and called the Wildlife Refuge Center in Lewiston. He arranged to rush the owl over and for them to be prepared to try to save the beautiful little guy. It was pitifully ill.

Head Chief left right away as our current business was finished anyway and Blackstone could take me home or I could walk from the Fire Hall. Blackstone loved animals and made "Whyte" promise to let her know the condition of the "victim" when he had some info. To ease her mind, I promised to put a reminder in the next community newsletter about this being a certified organic county and the Spotted Owl was on the federal near endangered species list. I wrote the newsletter quarterly. The many folks that didn't live here full time, even the residents that lived here year-round, but deliberately didn't get much news, seemed to enjoy the information focused on our specific community.

We were certain that we had everything done in case we were mobilized or 'called out', we locked down the Fire Hall and Blackstone dropped me off at my driveway gate. She was upset about the poisoning incident and wanted me to issue a warning to the guy. It really wasn't my jurisdictional authority. She was a strong woman that I have seen rappel down a steep hill and rescue victims from car wreaks; cut up a big tree fallen across the road with her gigantic chainsaw that she kept in her truck; and other feats of survival skills, but her soft heart for animals was widely known. I was concerned that she might go give the little city schoolteacher a piece of her mind so I promised to handle it if she would leave it be.

It was sometimes difficult to keep peace among neighbors who were in these isolated parts for different reasons and entirely unrelated goals. However, this was law and he needed to conform to the conservationists' mindset up here as the loggers had found out. At one time the logging industry had 17 mills operating in the county and they were clear cutting the area mercilessly until the early 1990s. They were destroying Northern Spotted Owl habitats.

The Northern Spotted Owl is one of three spotted owl subspecies. It is a medium-sized dark brown owl native to the Pacific Northwest. An important indicator species, the Northern Spotted Owl remains threatened due to continued population decline from human-caused habitat destruction and competition with invasive species, its main competitor is the barred owl. Most spotted owls inhabit federal lands (Forest Service, Bureau of Land Management, and National Park Service lands), although significant numbers occur on state lands in Washington, Oregon, and California, as well as tribal and private properties. The Northern Spotted Owl is intolerant of habitat disturbance. Each nesting pair needs a large amount of land for hunting and nesting. They will not migrate unless they experience drastic seasonal changes, such as heavy snows, which make hunting difficult.

In 1990, the logging industry estimated up to 30,000 of 168,000 jobs would be lost because of the owl's status, which agreed closely with a Forest Service estimate. Harvests of timber in the Pacific Northwest were reduced by 80%, decreasing the supply of lumber and increasing prices. However, jobs were already declining because of dwindling old-growth forest harvests and automation of the lumber industry. The county was down to 3 sawmills now, only one operating full time.

The controversy pitted individual loggers and small sawmill owners against environmentalists. Bumper stickers reading Kill a Spotted Owl—Save a Logger and I Like Spotted Owls—Fried appeared to support the loggers. Plastic spotted owls were hung in effigy in Oregon sawmills. The logging industry, in response to continued bad publicity, started the Sustainable Forestry Initiative. While timber interests and conservatives have cited the Northern Spotted Owl as an example of excessive or misguided environmental protection, many environmentalists view the owl as an "indicator species," or "canary in a coal mine" whose preservation has created protection for an entire threatened ecosystem. Protection of the owl, under both the Endangered Species Act and the National Forest Management Act, has led to significant changes in forest practices in the northwest.

I decided to ask Joe and Susan Bower to write an article for our upcoming quarterly newsletter for an update analysis on the progress of our efforts at preservation and habitat conservation for endangered species. The Bowers would have a handle on the scientific data and how to interpret it more than I would. Access to their expertise was good fortune for our community so I tapped them as a resource whenever we needed. They always responded. The Watershed Research and Training Center was another source of good data and expertise. Once we got this funding from the Fire Chiefs Association, I planned to partner with them for staffing, such as their wildlife biologist, as well as, their conservation expertise on the largest and most scientifically data-driven part of the Stewardship and Fire Mitigation projects. A wildlife biologist will look at things like how the Barred Owls have encroached on Northern Spotted Owl territory in the last several decades and are outcompeting them in many ways, adding to the existential pressure the Northern Spotted Owls face. Barred owls are ferocious predators that can move into habitats faster than prey can adapt, potentially triggering a trophic cascade, an ecosystem- wide shift. This was part of my Stewardship plan that was prepared with the help of the Bowers and the Watershed

Research Training Center.

These were my thoughts as I strolled down my long driveway to my house. Whenever I have an unusual encounter with wildlife in the area, I give it some thought and try to place its significance and symbolism. It seems that the sick owl's timing was perfect because he appeared when Jesse was there to immediately take him to get medical care at the Wildlife Refuge, which was near his home, so he knew the folks there. I felt certain that the little Spotted Owl would get the best attention possible. They would save it if they could. Poisoning was a serious condition, but I didn't want to start a war in the neighborhood so I'm thinking my plan for putting out some educational information, using the Bowers' data and knowledge would work. I felt better about that by the time I reached the house and Chez noticed my approach. She came bounding towards me, but stopped before she started her usual goofy greeting dance. She sniffed me very carefully and looked at me with concern in her soulful eyes. I knew she smelled the sick bird. After all, she was a bird dog even if she didn't like close contact with them. I smiled as I patted her head and told her what happened. She seemed to understand and walked along side me somberly as if she was really worried about a friend. It was very touching to me and confirmed that Chez was a highly sensitive creature.

Momma and Pete were anxious for a report. I reassured them that the fire was going away from us and while not under control, the resources were there to get it out.

Pete said he'd already loaded some things into the van and the construction camper, where Chez slept now. It was still usable to store things that we would need if we had to evacuate suddenly. I told them both that the Incident Commander had assured me that the fire was moving away from Dubakella Mountain. The weather reports favored us as far as wind direction. Of course, it doesn't hurt to have your ducks in a row. Fires are unpredictable and Pete was a man who did not like to get caught out short. He'd left the boat hooked to the truck, just in case. He could use the van to pull the camper. If we had to evacuate, I would most likely be at the Command Center. Momma would have to handle one of the vehicles. Momma considered herself an excellent driver and loved driving trucks and large vehicles. We once moved Aunt Lee from New Jersey to Florida with just Momma doing all the driving. She said she didn't think I could handle a large van. Another reason she was surprised at the thought of me handling a fire engine. I assured her that, indeed, I was a licensed certified emergency vehicle operator.

Pete asked me to come out to the powerhouse with him so he could show me something. I knew he wanted to get me alone and when we got out there, he said, "Mele called. He is coming up here tomorrow. He says he wants to see his grandmother before she leaves. I haven't told your mother because I assumed you'd want to do that. However, I did speak to Terry, his counselor, just to make sure that he had legitimate permission to come. He confirmed Mel has permission to come here."

I sighed, "If it's not one thing, it's another. How are you feeling about this?"

He shrugged resignedly, like what can we do. My son, Mele or Mel for short, was a disabled veteran who had run the gamut of vets going off the rails. He'd dropped out of college, joined the Marine Corp at the urging of his 18-year-old girlfriend, who he then married right out of basic training. After 5 years in the Corp, he had come back from the wars in the middle east seemingly undamaged, until it was time for him to function in everyday society; as a husband, father, employee, family member and person who could care for himself over a stretch of more than six months. His decline into alcoholism, drug addiction, thievery, domestic abuse, violence, incarceration, homelessness, poor health at the physical, mental, and emotional level has been one of the biggest and scariest nightmares of my life. Pete has been with me to every jail or prison he's been in.

Pete and I have been married 12 years. We got married a month before Mel went off to college, so this roller coaster, spiraling journey with my son is something that Pete has experienced with me every step of the way. We've tried to shield Momma from it but she raised five sons and some of it she has already guessed. However, I don't think she knows just how bad it has gotten before and since his divorce. He was now in his second rehab program through the church. He was in the program in the city of Sacramento and when that failed after several months, they gave him another chance at the facility in Cottonwood which was much more rural and closer to us by about two hours. He seemed to thrive in the more rural setting because he liked physical work. This place was a ranch.

We were always nervous because we never knew what could trigger something that could cause a relapse. Once Mel and I stopped into a fast-food restaurant to grab a quick lunch. It was a chain that neither of us had been to before, so we decided to go in and check out the menu more closely. We were in line, and he started to say he felt sick. Suddenly he ran out into the parking lot and vomited in the grass. When I got him in the car, he was hyperventilating so bad, I thought he would need CPR. He kept motioning for me to drive away from the place. We got a few blocks away and I pulled over just to make sure he was alright because he had his head out the window taking big gulps of air. He told me that whatever they were cooking or whatever oil they were using in the restaurant smelled like the burn pits that he and his fellow Marines endured in 'Desert Shield/Desert Storm'. He always used the name of the war or 'operation', like some folks say Vietnam or 'Nam. Mele said there was a bad feeling that the smell set off for him. He wanted me to drop him off at the park so he could walk around, breathe in some fresh air, and think. I didn't want to do it, but he's a grown man. He would have just gotten out of the car anyway.

He disappeared for weeks after that incident but called me once to say he was okay and not to worry about him. He finally turned up in Denver when he called Roadie, my lifelong friend, in the middle of the night and asked her to pick him up at a convenience store where his friend, the driver/owner of the car he was in, had been arrested for shoplifting. Roadie's family was old Colorado with some of them in prominent positions in local law enforcement.

She spoke to an officer on the scene, who knew Roadie's people and had heard of Roadie. She let her pick him up at the store. It probably would not have gone down that way if Mele didn't look more white or Polynesian than black plus Roadie is white. Let's face it, black men don't get grace from the law. Also, Roadie is well-known in the area for her work with abused, abandoned, and troubled juveniles. She founded and ran a large private agency that placed these kids in specialized homes. She'd even spoken at the United Nation's World Health Organization about trafficked children and how to foster parent and work with them.

It was fortuitous that he got a female officer who was sympathetic. He was a very handsome man who could be quite charming and even sincerely convincing. While he had his issues, he was not stupid or without merit. Also, he was willing to show his vulnerabilities to those that he thought would be empathetic. In other words, if I'm being honest, he knew how to work women, which I see as an inherited trait and a learned skill.

Momma was putty in his hands and, as for myself, Pete said I was easy pickings for Mel. While it's true, I love him with all my heart, the circumstances of his birth and early entry into my life, as well as, his persona, had created difficulties that I spent many years trying to get a handle on. This may sound vague. I find motherhood has many joys, but the hardships are epic. Once Pete and I moved up to the mountains, I have found a peace of mind from the cares of motherhood that I didn't expect to ever have once Mele was born into my life. It has been more of an acceptance of the karmic soul cycle that the natural world holds and is reflected in the spiritual realm as well, kind of a trophic-like pyramid.

I've had to dig deep into my heart, mind, soul, and collective subconscious to find what is a simple answer, Love and Ohm Tao. Each of us must find our way and accept the path that those in our life chose to work out their own soul and life's Gordian Knot.

I went back in the house and told my mother, "Mele is coming up the mountain."

Chapter 18

A Mighty Long Way

Momma

Hope could tell that Roadie wasn't angry. She was stressed out. She was now tasked with packing up the apartment on her own. Egg and Carter had eloped, and she was traveling with him. Hope was in a bad situation and couldn't leave the islands.

Roadie had decided to go back to Colorado to finish her masters' degree in sociology and none of us were there to help her. She said that the guys babysitting my beautiful blue meat Persian cat, Luv, would be happy to keep her. My expensive, commercial grade bowls, crockery and cookware were with the couple that was running my organic baking business. She was boxing up Egg's painting and sculpting studio plus my albums and instruments for Egg and Carter to take. Carter was paying for movers to come in once she had things sorted to go. She was giving everything else to the Digger Store and the nearly brakeless pink Cadillac that we tooled around the City in was going to another group of girlfriends who shared a house and was part of our circle. Hope was actually feeling very unsettled with Roadie and Egg leaving this serene home in the City, which had been her anchor or base. She was feeling a lot like her poem, A Rootless Root.

Hope was waiting for results from the gynecologist that Doc had arranged for her to see. It was nerve racking. Deana was acting a little distant towards Hope since the Wick fiasco. They were all at Doc's place in Honaunau. Hope was still staying with Doc in Puako. Godwin was talking about leaving the Big Island and going back home to Canada, most likely Victoria, or an island near there, so he could still work restoring boats and sculpt, too. Apparently, he'd lived in the area before and had friends who supported his craft. Deana, who clearly had a jealous streak, thought it was a woman that he wanted to return to there. They were in a turmoil because she didn't want to go or leave Hawaii.

Tab was moving to Maui where a friend had a studio for him to live and work in remote Ulupalakua, which would be an idyllic setting for this great talented, reclusive Rapidograph artist. Deana said she just might go with him to Maui. Grady, who had inherited family money, said he was going on a trek to Thailand to clear his head. Hope felt that she had attracted a predatory spirit into their midst and the energy had torn their peaceful little enclave apart. However, it was hard for her focus on anything other than her own precarious situation. She couldn't go back to her place in the City and her little safety net of friends here in the islands was falling apart. She had missed her period, and her breast were feeling enlarged. She hoped it was just a reaction to being late. She wouldn't know because her menstrual cycle was so regular. All she could wish and pray for was that the results of the tests were negative. The doctor said to give them a couple of weeks and the lab would mail the test results directly to her. She could call if she had questions.

Doc had told Hope that she needed to stop worrying before she loses her mind. He'd been trying to get her to sing or work on her music, but she was paralyzed with anxiety. While Hope felt certain he was trying to help. Doc was trying to take her mind off the circumstances. He had even gone so far as to book her an 'audition' with a band on Maui at the Happy Valley Music Commune. It was run, as far as communes are run, by his close friend, who was a music event promoter. Hope was so worried that she got little joy from the whole scene. She noticed the promoter's wife seemed to be doing most of the real work of keeping the place going and everyone fed.

The Happy Valley Band was the warmup group for whatever name acts the promoter brought to Maui for his rock concerts, which were mainly held outdoors. Hope did not vibe well with the drummer, a black guy named Lloyd Earle, a very flamboyant character who dressed all in purple. Also, all the songs that the band played were male oriented and done in strictly hard rock genre. Hope was uncomfortable singing Muddy Water's version of *I'm A Man!**

Deana and Tab came to Happy Valley when they got to Maui to see her, but it was mostly to visit the promoter's wife, who everyone knew and loved. She'd had a dress shop in town that Deana had done some original designs for and that had sold well. Everyone throughout the artistic island community knew Tab for his intricate pen and ink Rapidograph posters and drawings. While it was good to be with them again, there was still some distance. Although Hope was put in an impossibly awkward situation all the way around, she didn't know how to fix it.

She told Doc that she didn't want to sing with this band. He still tried to talk her into it so she acquiesced and did a gig with the group at the opening of a new restaurant on the beach. It was the worst set she'd ever had with a band. She was practically booed off stage and Lloyd Earle played his drums so loud that she was drowned out during most of the loud set anyway. Her type of style and voice was too sultry and subtle for this type of band. She angrily demanded that Doc take her back to the Big Island and that she gets paid some money for the humiliation.

Since they got back from Maui, Hope had been anxiously watching for the little jeep that brought the mail every day. She knew her fate was coming. Doc's house was at the end of the street, so it seemed to take all day for them to get the mail to his place. It was almost five o'clock and the mail was just getting to the house. Hope waited until she couldn't hear the noisy little Jeep's motor before she walked out the mailbox. There was a letter there with her name on it addressed in care of Doc. It was from the lab. She anxiously tore open the envelop. The report from the lab said it was positive that she was pregnant, but it didn't list any venereal disease, which the doctor had also tested her for. Hope stood in the middle of the driveway like a lost deer in headlights. She didn't know what to do or where to go. The sea called her. She walked blindly towards the sound, but she was sobbing so hard that she stumbled and fell in the sandy grass. She curled up in a ball and cried until her body was racked with shivers.

Then she seemed to travel on an astral plane back to New York City. It was dark and raining and she was flying over the city. She looked down and saw a man staggering down the sidewalk. He stepped into the quiet street without looking, just as a cab came careening around the poorly lit corner. The cab clipped him and knocked into the gutter where he smashed his head hard on the concrete curb and died on the spot. The driver didn't seem to realize that he had just hit a man and kept right on going. Hope had lost a very close boyfriend this way. In fact, a man that she had loved, but couldn't consider marrying because he had some issues with addiction that he always seemed to be working on. He was a New York City 'trust fund baby', meaning his great grandfather had made a lot of money and left him a chunk of change. He'd been a well educated, but down to earth intellectual. However, Hope had learned the downside of that high intellect once he started using drugs again and she wanted no part of it. It was very disappointing to see him so weakened.

One day she'd come to his apartment and used her key when he didn't answer the door. He was overdosed in the bathroom. She had to revive him and call an ambulance, saving his life. After that she applied for and got a job that would take her away from the relationship, as well as offered her an opportunity to travel. She was hired at a major airline as one of their very first black stewardesses. She had to leave Rutgers University to do it. She wanted to see where the opportunity would take her. At that point, Hope had never even taken an airline flight. They never asked her that question.

She knew she couldn't stay in New York because her love for him would be her undoing and she just couldn't short shrift her own life that way. When he died, she felt it in her spirit because she had loved him. Hope thought reincarnation was a real possibility. It was as if this sudden vision seemed to tell her that the entity in her body was a soul connected to this man, Sunny, who she had once loved so deeply.

She had a lot of disparate thoughts lying there in that yard, from calling on her mother, sister, aunt, and ancestors to help her, to realizing that, indeed, she had to face her fate. Hope couldn't be sure how long she was there. It was dark when she opened her eyes to Doc calling her name with his car lights shining on her prone body. He got her up, put her in the car and drove right up to the door so he could get her in the house.

She kept saying Sunny's name over and over. Doc tried to question her to find out who Hope was talking about. She was very incoherent when she tried to explain what her vision had shown her. He just wanted her to rest. She seemed dehydrated so he opened a coconut that he had on the lanai and gave her fresh coconut water to help replenish her electrolytes. He had her smoke some strong pakalolo to get her to quiet down and sleep.

Doc had been working all day and he was hungry. He went into the kitchen once Hope was resting and started preparing some steak to grill. He knew Hope ate little or no meat, but she was going to eat this tonight because she was weak, anemic, recovering from dehydration and pregnant. He was determined to nurse her back to health and then get her to marry him. He realized that she was young enough to be his daughter. There was a 20-year age gap. He loved and cared about her. Plus, her options were now limited.

He would present his proposal as an in or out situation. Frankly, he thought he'd been a good friend to her. She could do worse than him. He could offer her a good, secure, and interesting lifestyle that would broaden her horizons and lend some stability to a pregnant unwed young black woman. She was an independent sort of girl though and he was not sure that he could persuade her even in her reduced circumstance. One other caveat that he offered her was protection from Wick. If Hope was his wife, Wick would not dare lay a hand on her again.

The smell of cooking wafted from the grill on the lanai into the house. Hope was awake and hungry. She felt like she was in a stupor. She could barely move because she didn't feel like she was in control of her senses. She still felt like she was having the same out of body experience that she had in the yard. She heard Doc bustling around in the kitchen and forced herself to get up and use the bathroom. She took a brief shower and put on a fresh pair of shorts and t-shirt. She went into the kitchen only to find Doc on the lanai where he had set the long table out there with an arrangement of fresh Red Lehua Blossoms.

The Hawaiian Islands are filled with an amazing number of plants, trees, and flowers. Much of the flora is incredibly colorful and beautiful, some of it is tied to ancient Hawaiian lore. This is especially true in the case of the Red Lehua Blossom that grows on the Ohia Tree. Both the Lehua and the Ohia are plants that can be found in many places on the islands. The Ohia can grow as both a shrub and a tall tree. According to ancient Hawaiian legend, there is a much bigger back story to how the Lehua blossom and Ohia tree came about. Ohia was a human man at one point, a man that Pele, the Volcano Goddess of Fire, had her eye on. Pele wanted Ohia, but Ohia had his heart set on Lehua, who was also in love with him. Pele wasn't big on being rejected by Ohia, so she transformed Ohia into a twisted mess of a tree. Lehua was devastated and begged Pele to reverse the spell, but Pele refused. Lehua didn't give up and begged other Gods for help. They agreed that the two lovers (Lehua and Ohia) should be together forever so they transformed Lehua into the red flower now known as the Lehua Blossom. Ever since that happened, it's said that the Ohia tree has bloomed with beautiful Lehua blossoms.

Hope told Doc that the arrangement was lovely and that she knew the lore around the blooms. He gave her one of his sardonic smiles and motioned for her to sit at the table.

"I know you don't do much meat. I want to advise you that you're in a weakened state and this is as good as it gets for steak. This is fresh from the Parker Ranch store, just up the road in Waimea. The Ranch also supplies hand selected animals for its retail grass fed, branded beef program, which can be found locally in Hawaii grocery stores under the Paniolo Cattle Company brand. Parker Ranch cattle graze year-round on forage that is healthy and plentiful. Parker Ranch is one of the largest and oldest producers of natural, pasture raised cattle in the nation. Most of their calves are exported to the mainland to be grown out on grass and finished for market. Parker Ranch is committed to preserving the Paniolo or Hawaiian cowboy culture and legacy by operating a sustainable cattle business on 130,000 acres of rich natural volcanic grasslands, on the slopes of the Mauna Kea and Kohala Mountains. I know you haven't explored this area much yet. Cattle is king around here. Richard Smart, who is a direct descendent of Mr. Parker and his Hawaiian Ali'i wife and a friend of mine, plans to keep it that way."

While he was giving her the history of the meal, he sat a wonderful looking steak in front of her along with grilled vegetables and a large picture of ice water with lemon. Hope was famished and it smelled so good. First, she drank a big glass of water and told Doc that she was grateful for everything that he'd done for her. She said that she was humbled in the face of his kindness. They ate in contented silence for awhile, savoring the delicious food and ignoring the big problematic elephant in the room. She didn't want to spoil the dinner which he'd made really romantic by lighting candles for the table, tiki torches were burning in the backyard, and he'd turned on string lights around the lanai.

Hope knew Doc had feelings for her and she really cared about him. He was clearly an old-fashioned romantic. He was turning on his considerable charm tonight. When they finished eating, he wouldn't let Hope do the dishes. She helped clean off the table. They sat on the couch in the living room holding hands quietly and listened to soothing Hawaiian slack key playing low, with the waves in the background.

"Hope, I think we should get married. Before you answer, hear me out. I know you care about me, but you are not in love with me. I feel confident that love will come."

Doc made a strong case. He talked about her situation and how he could protect her and her child from the 'sire', which is how he referred to Wick. Hope was grateful for his candor, which was a trait that she liked in him. He told her that he didn't want to have more children, but if they were married, he'd declare paternity for her child. That would offer her legal protections from anything Wick might try.

He said, "Listen, this is 1968. We are supposed to be in the Age of Aquarius where folks are more enlightened, but there is still a whole social system out there that clings to norms and traditions. This means ours would not be an easy marriage because of our clear differences in everything; race, age and more hidden things like financial status and religion. I am not a practicing Jew, but it is part of my culture. What I'm asking you would require you to be all the way in or all the way out. We've been in limbo until we could find out whether you were pregnant or not. Now we know which means that there are some decisions that only you can make. I'd like to be an option that you consider. I want to be in your life, as your husband not just a friend."

Hope was quiet for a while as she contemplated this fateful day and proposal. She kept reliving her vision of Sunny. She decided to explain to him the deeply secret significance of this visitation. She thought he was under the illusion that she was an innocent young thing. She may as well be as honest with him as he was being with her.

"Doc, I'm not as innocent or naive as you seem to think I am. Yes, I'm just 22, but I've lived on my own in New York City, mostly in the Village, since I graduated early from high school. Then, the airline based me in San Francisco, so I moved to the Haight.

You can image that I have met and dealt with some interesting people and circumstances.

I never explained to you why I came on this 'holoholo' to Hawaii with Deana. Sunny was a man that I had a deep love relationship with. As it turned out, he had a prior 'luv' that he didn't tell me about until it was too late. The day I found out about it was one of the worse days of my life. It was the day that my doctor told me I was pregnant.

I excitedly rushed to his apartment to tell him because I was really a dumb nineteen-year-old. When I let myself in with the key he'd given me, I found him on the floor in his bathroom overdosed with a needle sticking out of his arm. It was a true nightmare. I managed to get him into the cold shower and revive him. I knew he'd once been an addict, but he'd gone to one of the best rehab programs in the world. I thought he had been clean since I'd met him. The ambulance took him to the hospital and other hospital stays followed.

He had an inheritance so the trust could afford to take care of his needs. However, I did not want his child or the long-term consequences of dealing with Sunny's addiction. Either I was too selfish or too young or too much like my mother, who refused to marry my Dad because of his alcoholism. Instead, Momma had a child out of wedlock in times of stricter social mores than now. Anyway, I called my cousin who was a practical nurse, and she knew an RN who could help me. In other words, I went and got a 'back alley' abortion.

Even though, Sunny was going through his own struggles with heroin, I made him go with me to get the abortion. I stayed at his apartment right afterwards. This turned out to be a good thing because he lived in a pretty ritzy area of the upper east side of Manhattan. When I was about to bleed to death, they sent an ambulance quickly and took me to the hospital. Although, they would not take me to the nearest one, but up to Harlem, when they saw I was a black girl. The wait at the emergency room almost killed me. Sunny, using his well-known family name, got me admitted and treated. I had to sign documents saying I had received an abortion. When I woke up from surgery the next morning, two FBI agents at my bed side were trying to question me, demanding to know who had given me the abortion. I guess the night before, I had said that the abortion was given to me in New Jersey, which made it an interstate crime. The FBI was called. What they didn't know was that Sunny was still at the hospital.   When he caught them at my bedside, he raised holy hell and called his aunt, who was a big deal at the Justice Department. His was a family full of silk-stocking attorneys, but his aunt was a well-known scraper. She got the FBI off our backs. They never contacted me again.

We stayed in touch some after I moved west, but he was killed in a hit and run accident. His aunt was the one who called me to break the news. I had already been living in San Francisco for over a year when it happened. I knew something was wrong even before that phone call came through. I had tried to call him a few days earlier. At that point, I was in another steady relationship, but Sunny's death set me back.

I became essentially grief stricken so the relationship ended. Deana witnessed most of it, so she wanted me to get away for a break from the 'karmic wheel' as she called it. What she didn't know is that you can't run from yourself. When you found me tonight, I'd had a vision about him. It was tonight, right?

Because time is acting weird to me right now. The vision revealed that he was the soul that I was carrying in my body. I cannot reject him but must give him life and love him as my child. Of course, I don't see any other alternative no matter how difficult the journey. Here I am now trying to keep my sins contained in a safe environment. I am not going through another nightmare that is abortion.   My first priority is the safety of my child. This goal will have to be my main concern. Everything else is secondary.

Now that you know about my past, if you still want to marry me, the answer is yes. You know the reason why. I hope a romance will grow. Right now, the truth will have to be enough. Now, the question is are you 'all in or out'?"

"Hope, nobody can sing the blues like you and not understand some Universal Truths. I am feeling like the luckiest guy in the world, and we've never even seen each other naked," he chuckled. They both fell over each other laughing.

They married a few weeks later at the tiny little church in Puako. Doc knew the minister who ran it from his larger congregation in Waimea. They asked Viv and Ted to stand with them as witnesses. Viv played her silver flute for Hope's short walk down the aisle. Afterwards, the four went for a quiet, lavish lunch on the patio at the Mauna Kea Beach Resort nearby. Doc surprised them when he borrowed Viv's flute to serenade his new bride. Everyone clapped because he was an accomplished flutist. Ted looked at Hope and shrugged like - who knew? Doc explained that when he was a child, before fleeing to America, he'd been given tutoring lessons in classical music and the silver flute was his instrument of choice; even though right now, he only had a large bamboo one.

They ended their lovely day with a romantic afternoon of sexual pleasure at the hotel. It was the first time that they were together in that way. Hope was self conscious because she was showing. She had only gained weight in her stomach and breast so she may have felt heavy, but she wasn't. Doc was kind and gentle. Hope was ready for the physical contact because the pregnancy made her horny. She enjoyed his skilled love making plus he was well endowed, a pleasant surprise. It was a lovely day of love.

It was a lovely day until night fell and Doc made them some Magic Mushroom tea. To Hope's surprise Viv had let Doc borrow her flute. He started playing out on the lanai. Hope, who was really zonked from the tea, was in the bathtub for what seemed like hours finally heard banging on their door. By the time, she managed to get out of the tub and put on the lush hotel terry cloth robe, it had stopped. She heard voices on the lanai. She went to see what was happening. She was stunned to see Brah-la standing there in a suit, with another guy in a security uniform, talking to Doc. When Brah-la saw Hope, he tried to hide his astonishment. He had not seen her, nor had she been seen out and about in a public way, since the nasty incident at Akamai Barnes.

Doc ordered groceries for delivery. She had mostly been resting and writing in isolation at his place since they came back from Maui. She was definitely showing signs of the impregnation. He explained to Hope that he was now head of security at the resort.

He'd moved into a house in Puako since he and Jackie got married. He said the guests were complaining about the noise. Doc would have to stop playing outside for tonight. Doc was having none of it and acting quite belligerent, but Hope got him to agree to stop until morning. When Brah-la left, he turned on Hope, gave her a blistering speech about taking his side no matter what. He kept yelling, "In or out!"

Hope was feeling the effects of the psychedelic and couldn't stand the vibe. She ran out the back door onto the lanai and down towards the beach. She fell halfway there and couldn't get up as she lay there sobbing hysterically. That's where Brah-la found her.

He helped her get back to the room and told them that they would have to leave the resort. Doc was furious. Brah-la was a bit larger than Doc and he had the authority to put them out. He said he would drive them back to Puako and have the concierge service deliver their car and bags to their home later. It was a shoddy end to what had been a lovely day. Brah-la took them home and came in to make sure they were alright.

Hope was not very lucid until the next day. She'd taken LSD in the Haight and other organic psychedelics. She now started to wonder how it would affect the child she was carrying. She also wondered why Doc had given her the tea. They had never indulged together before. She did not like the person that she saw on the mushrooms. He frightened her and made her feel like she'd married a Dr. Jekyll and Mr. Hyde. Now, she started to wonder what she had let herself in for. She lay quietly in bed next to him until he stirred then she popped up, quickly eased into the bathroom, and put on some clothes.

She walked out to the beach before he could say anything to her. She came back an hour later feeling refreshed. He was in the kitchen with coffee. Hope poured her a cup, sat down across from him and they stared at each other for awhile.

He finally shrugged and said, "In or out?"

Hope knew then that this was his way of manipulating her. She almost threw the coffee in his face, but violence was not the way to handle these circumstances. She said, "I want my mother here for the birth. Will that be alright with you?"

"That would be great!" He said gleefully, but he'd never met or even spoken to 'Alley Cat' so he had no idea what Hope was asking or why. He just thought she was saying that she was in and having her mother come was part of the bargaining agreement.

However, he would find out that she had a bigger backbone than he ever knew. Hope felt a little like she'd jumped from the frying pan to the fire, but she was no victim. She knew that she'd made a bargain that was either with a devil or a saint. Time would tell and her Momma could bring pressure to bear on that clock.

Doc had a surprise too, he said, "I am glad that you want your mother to come when the baby is born because I need to go to Hong Kong. There is a conference that I've been invited to attend with Dr. Weaver. We'll get to discuss some of our theories on treating returning Vietnam Vets.

Because it was happening around the time of the birth, I had not committed, but this may work out well. I'll buy your mother's ticket based on when the conference takes place and leave the return open so she can go back whenever you don't need her help anymore.

Have you spoken to her; do you know if she's available to be away from home for a bit?"

Hope's mother was in rare form when she spoke to her the next day, while Doc was at his office. She was angry with Hope for not telling her about the wedding and now the pregnancy too. Hope felt chastised. She built Doc up like he was so great without revealing the things that she knew her mother would discern as flaws, like his age, race, religion, and temperament. When she heard he was a doctor and that he was affiliated with Dr. Weaver, whose family my mother knew, she calmed down and said she would come for the birth.

Hope's mother was a very straight forward woman. She sat out on Doc's lanai and told him just what she thought of his marrying Hope. She expressed contempt at a man older than she was "taking advantage of a girl young enough to be his daughter".

She asked him if he deliberately got Hope pregnant to trap her into a "May/December" thing. Doc took it like a champ and never defended himself by revealing the situation that Hope was in when he married her. However, he was glad to get on the plane for Hong Kong the next day. He didn't want to tangle with 'Alley Cat' more than necessary.

He knew Hope didn't want her mother to know the truth about the pregnancy, so he kept his mouth shut, which was the bargain that he'd promised. Her mother would not be there that long after he returned. He'd made sure of that when he booked her ticket. The woman was a nightmare to reason with and she did not like him. She'd even said that he should have married her because she was in his age category. While it was true that she was two years younger and still a good-looking woman, he thought that was just nasty of her to say to his face, in his own home. As far as he was concerned, he was glad she lived 6,000 miles away. If this trip to Hong Kong worked out, he planned to put even more distance between her and his new wife. He loved Hope, but he knew there were things and flaws about him that she would eventually question. He held no illusions about that - psychology was his area of expertise and he was not above using it to keep his wife in check. He knew her mother could put a glitch in his way of doing things. This was not his first marriage and he liked to keep the upper hand with the women in his life. His biggest concern with Hope was that she was strongwilled.

Now he knew that came from her mother. To keep her with him, he'd have to use his own methods. He'd lost one wife to an unwanted divorce. He didn't want to go through that again. He planned to put his considerable skills in play to keep this woman in check. What worried him is that she may have figured that out since their wedding night. She was not as open with him since the psilocybin trip. He knew he should not have tested their bond so soon, especially since she was pregnant. A much more reserved Hope seemed to tip toe around him. They'd had a good friendship and he wanted that again too. He planned to work on that when he got back from Hong Kong. This was an important trip for him. He didn't want to be distracted with concern about his marriage to Hope. Her mother might be a problem. If everything went well at the conference, he had a fix for that. The baby would be here soon. Hope would be even more dependent on him. She would have to go along with his plans whether she liked them or not.

Hope's mother liked to walk on the beach. She did it regularly in Florida where she lived so they drove the short distance to Hapuna Beach each morning, strolled around for a bit until Hope begged to go back home. She was carrying 35 pounds of extra weight and on her small frame it was uncomfortable. One day they were at the beach and Hope saw Jackie was walking along the water's edge. She realized that Jackie was pregnant too. They hugged each other and chatted excitedly about getting together on the beach regularly to walk. Hope's mother liked Jackie right away and asked her a lot of questions.   Jackie was married to Brah-la now and knew how to keep her mouth shut and answer, but not reveal, so Hope felt that she'd made a friend that she could trust with her secret. She felt certain that Brah-la had guessed at what happened between her and Wick and probably told Jackie. In any case, they started meeting each morning for their shared walks. They were both expecting to give birth about the same time. They talked mostly baby stuff because they were due to become new mothers any day. Jackie's mother had passed away at an early age so she kind of took to Hope's mother and queried her on all kinds of worries about child rearing. Hope started to notice other women at the beach with very young children and realized other young families were in the area. She had not really been getting out and about since Maui and the wedding. She had been keeping to the little rocky beach across the street from Doc's house when she wanted to be close to the ocean. It was reassuring that other mothers were around.

Jackie told them about her friend's cute little shop in Honokaa that had some nice baby things, so Hope's mother wanted to go there. They took a trip up the hill through Waimea and into Honokaa, known as the Nut Capital of the World, because they grow lots of macadamia nuts there. It took less than an hour and it was a good sightseeing outing for both. Hope had basically been locked down for months. Doc's car was the only transportation they had so she just contented herself with giving him shopping lists and ordering grocery deliveries on his account from the market in Waimea. She still had a little money coming in from her business partners in San Francisco. It was not a lot, but Doc paid for everything. He was generous towards her so she could not fault him for that, but she liked her independence and planned to get back to work in some capacity once the baby was old enough.   She   told   her mother this, who said she was crazy to rush back to work. 'Alley Cat' said to her, "It's better to be an old man's darling than a young man's fool!"

Honokaa is a quaint town with a gorgeous view of the Pacific Ocean. They were having a lovely mother/daughter day browsing the shops, buying baby things and then they had a nice leisurely sit-down lunch. Hope started to feel uncomfortable after she ate, but that was normal lately. When the first pain hit her, she yelped a little. Her mother was at the counter paying the bill, so she didn't hear her, and the pain subsided. As they were strolling to the car another sharp pain almost buckled her knees. She grabbed her mother by hand and said she thought she might be going into labor. Her mother turned her around and they went back into the restaurant. She had them call an ambulance. Hope was taken to the little local hospital in Honokaa. Her mother followed the ambulance in the car. She had been driving anyway because Hope was not up to it. Her driver's license from California had expired on her birthday nearly nine months back. She had not bothered to renew it because Doc did all the driving. It was his car not hers.

Hope spent the next ten hours in the most excruciating pain she could imagine. She wanted natural birth so refused any drugs. When her OB/Gyn finally arrived, her mother had a few choice words for him. By that time a kindly nurse, of obvious Asian descent, had performed the miracle of a Shiatsu back rub on her, which relaxed her back and suddenly her water broke. They had to rush her into the delivery room. She was the only person in the hospital delivering a baby so there was easy availability for the delivery surgery.

When the baby was born, the doctor said, "Wow! Crème de Cacao. He's beautiful. You have a fine-looking son!"

Chapter 19

Out Lands: Living Off The Grid

Mele

From my upstairs window at my desk, I watched Mele coming down the driveway in his white Bronco II. I wondered if he had renewed his license. A mother's thought for a child who sometimes forgets "small" details. Of course, I reminded myself that he is not a child, but a grown man. Nevertheless, these are valid concerns for a loved one who has shown a distinct inability to keep his feet fully grounded in the minutiae of everyday life. Chez was going nuts because she recognized his vehicle. She adored and loved Mele. His goodness is deep because dogs, especially, love him.

Even dogs that don't take to people easily will roll over and show their underbellies for Mele. I knew that Chez would not leave his side as long as he was here. She would ignore me. He let her sleep in the bed with him and lounge all over him as much as she wanted. With me, Chez had to obey a few boundaries. Clearly, he was her favorite.

I walked down the stairs to find him and Momma hugging warmly. They really seemed to understand each other which was more than I could say for me with either of them. When he saw me, he came towards me with his arms open. I caught my breath at how handsome he was as he towered over me for one of his big bear hugs. Even as a baby, people would stop me at the market and exclaim over my beautiful golden boy.

As he grew up, though, he became prickly about folks commenting on his looks. He said it was because guys thought he was soft. He was not having it. He developed a tough exterior in his behavior. In his teens, I had him in session with psychologists. They claimed he was antisocial. He said he wasn't talking to any "white guys" about his feelings, and I should stop wasting money. He's had a mind of his own since he was a kindergartener.

It was a challenge being his mother in more ways than one. I never told him about Wick's behavior towards me. I just couldn't bring myself to explain it. Whenever, he'd ask me about Wick, I'd just say that it was my fault that I'd cut him out of our lives when he was a baby and never let him back in. He understood instinctively that I would not entertain any further conversation about it. One thing I can say, he has great instincts and is very empathetic to certain kinds of people. He can't abide bullies and that is what has gotten him into trouble with the law and society.

Pete was doing some coaching for the local high school, so he was in Hayfork, but he'd hooked the electricity and water lines up at the trailer that Mele stayed in, on our lot next door. Because we were on our own system for electricity, as well as, water and sewer, when he wasn't here with us, we kept the trailer closed to our systems. It had a composting toilet and closed drainage tank for the shower and sinks. I told him that his place was ready and if he wanted to go get settled, we would have dinner together a little later. He wanted to sit a while and talk, so the three of us got caught up on family members. Momma finally asked him how the program was going.

He couldn't avoid the elephant in the room any longer. This was hard for him because he was often evasive when it came to talking about his problems. In some ways, I was kind of surprised at his answer, and in other ways, I was not. He started talking about God, his faith and basically testifying about everything that has transpired since he returned from the war in the Middle East. Through all that he has endured, in terms of heart break, when his wife left him; heavy drug use and addiction to crack cocaine; poor health as a result of having Hepatitis C and Gulf War Syndrome;

incarceration for murder; he has always had faith that God would bring him out of it.

When he was a child, I put him in Christian schools, which were not always the best thing for him academically, but I wanted him to have a similar faith foundation like I was given. It sustained me in many ways through some rough places in my life. I thought it would be a refuge for him as well. I knew that his path would not be easy, if for no other reason, who fathered him. This was one of the ways that I thought he would be protected from darkness that can destroy one's soul. I felt certain I knew him from a previous life because of my vision early in the pregnancy and it was my job to give him a sense of faith to lean on, as my family had done for me. We never lived near Hardy Grove, my family church in North Carolina, but the spirit of that church was in my heart. I hoped he would get some of that from me.

One of the main reasons that I wanted to develop the land here in the mountains was to provide a sanctuary for Mele. He was just a toddler when I received the land. I always wanted to have a place where he could be away from the city and those kinds of influences. Of course, I learned that you can't run from your fate or karmic path. This "sanctuary" in these mountains was a chance for him to search for truth or salvation, which ever would be enough for him. He'd already lived through so much and he was not an old man. Having spent his formative years in Hawaii and the South Pacific, he loved music. We moved away to the 'mainland' when he was ten years old.

To lift the mood from the conversation or perhaps to gel his struggles into hope, I took my 12-string out of the case and tuned it up. Mele and I had a couple of songs that we sometimes sang together so I hit a few cords of one of his favorites, *I Shall Be Released**.

Mele went right into the song, with his soulful voice and the blues rhythms, it gave the tune a deeper feel and a more personal meaning than the original. When we finished, Momma broke out clapping.

Mele and I looked at each other and almost started crying because that song sustained us through his being jailed for murder. While it was self-defense, he still had to endure months of incarceration and uncertainty. I suffered the emotional trauma right along with him. My brother, who was a Marine too, encouraged us with the 'hood' mantra that, 'it's better to be judged by twelve than carried by six'. However, Mele had a hung jury the first time then a self-defense dismissal the second time around. It has been hard on me, as his mother, to watch him become downtrodden and depressed through these tribulations. Sometimes, though, he surprises me and finds a way to lift his own spirits. He seems to be in that cycle right now. We've had screaming fights that devolve into exhaustive, long discussions about his mental attitudes and behaviors.

Even he can't explain some of the disconnect that he has with everyday life tasks. Sometimes, I want to say to him that it's his DNA. However, I would really have to go into depth about what that meant to me because I knew that he would never accept anything less than the full explanation. The truth was that I had spent his whole life hiding the secret of his conception and birth origin. I was not sure that bringing it into light now that he was an adult would help him nor would it be fair, especially since he had his own troubled path to navigate these days. It was as difficult a decision as I have ever made, but I've stuck to it for all these years.

Once when he was first born and Momma saw that he didn't really favor Doc at all, she asked me about it and I countered with I thought he looked like my father, Dean. She kind of agreed with that so it put the conversation to rest for all these decades. Now every chance she gets, she comments on how much like Dean he looks and that he even walks like him.

When she says it, I always think, "Yeah, but he sounds and acts like Quick Wick." He sometimes speaks in a kind of staccato speech pattern that sounds just like Wick or he will laugh loudly like him. I have to turn around to make sure that the man is not in the same room with me.

Let me be the first to admit that it can be disconcerting. What I can I say is that I love my son, even if he sometimes reminds me of his 'sire'. I truly believe that I have shown only love to my child because that is all I have ever felt since I laid eyes on him the moment he was born.

I have never felt resentment towards him for his father's folly. His entrance into my life completely changed my trajectory and plans. I was unprepared, to say the least, for the burden of motherhood. I'm just glad I wasn't as young as my own mother when I became a parent. Even to this day, I have to be grateful to Doc for helping me when I was in a rather daunting circumstance. Our marriage didn't work out for some obvious reasons and even got a little ugly near the end, but it was the right thing for the time. Also, we eventually got our emotions under control, started acting like mature thinking adults and worked out a calm civilized way to end the union. It took a lot of tears to get there.

Momma even got involved all the way from Florida at one point, when I was trying to move out of the house with just a few things like, my clothes, my instruments, and some household items like, Mele's bed and a rocking chair that I'd had since he was born. Doc was so angry that he kept taking the things back in the house. My mother knew when I was moving out and anticipated some trouble.

She called Sheriff Abreu directly and asked him to send a squad car over to our house because she suspected domestic abuse. Evidently, she was very persuasive because he did send a Sheriff to the house, who stood by while I finished piling stuff on my new roommate's friend's truck. This was unexpected since Sheriff Abreu knew Doc personally and had worked with him on cases for the Health Department. When I asked Momma what she said to him, she wouldn't give me a straight answer. We all know how dramatic she could be so I can only guess that it was an exaggeration of the danger in the situation. My sister, Faith, said she told them to wail in the background like something terrible had happened to their family member. This is how she rolls when she wants her way. She dramatizes it to the max. Anyway, I never found out exactly how she worked it. Doc was very embarrassed by it all, which was never my intention. I just wanted to get out of the house and end our Faustian Bargain, now a control struggle between our two wills. It was not healthy for either of us, especially with Mele caught in the middle. It affected him too. Once I moved out, I saw a decidedly happier child. Of course, it helped that we moved a half block from a great beach so he could continue his water sports, like boogey boarding and snorkeling.

However, Doc took my mother's "interference" as an insult and did something that I never anticipated. If nothing else good came out of his actions, it taught me a valued lifelong lesson. He closed our joint savings account and took all the money. Most of it was money I had earned when we were overseas. All of expenses for housing, utilities and travel were paid for by his contract so we lived off his salary.

We paid the help, household expenses and vacations with his cash flow. I went to work too because we had a housekeeper and nanny for Mele. We saved my entire paycheck the whole time we were overseas. We had substantial savings when we returned to Hawaii. I had no idea whatsoever that he could just go into the bank and drain the account without my permission. The old fashioned, misogynistic, prejudice Japanese bank manager let him do it. I had no power to do anything about it at the time.

I learned to never, ever give anyone else control of my money. Before Pete and I got married, I made it clear that was non-negotiable for me. Pete was making much more money than I was, but it didn't matter. Managing my own financial affairs was mental and emotional security for me, after the really harrowing experience of being harshly cast into destitution by someone I trusted.

Fortunately, a friend of my roommate gave me a job at her wonderful company where I flourished. When she sold it, I used my contacts from my job there to step up my game and get a career job at an upbeat media company. I must think that, not only was it a lesson learned, but one that set me on the path to my financial wisdom and independence. Anyway, Mele, who has always been tuned into me, observed it all.

When he was young, Mele often brought the questions of life back to his lineage. He asked me how many parents it took to be born. I tried to explain it to him, but to my astonishment, he turned it into a math problem. It surprised me because his math skills were so sketchy that I had enrolled him at a math lab for tutoring. He said that when he tried to figure it out, he saw it like this, then he gave me a long math answer, "It takes 2 parents to be born, not counting bonus fathers; 4 grandparents; 8 great grandparents; 16 second great grandparents; 32 third great grandparents; 64 fourth great grandparents; 128 fifth great grandparents; 256 sixth great grandparents; 512 seventh great grandparents; 1,024 eighth great grandparents; 2, 048 ninth great grandparents, that's already 4,094 people. It's amazing that we found each other."

I just caught my breath and understood that this beautiful, odd mind was my son. The only thing I could do was love and protect his soul as long as I could. Perhaps, that was the message from his answering his own question. I don't know, but I did my best to grasp how to guide him to adulthood. Admittedly, I often felt ill- prepared to deal with his temperament, which included fits of anger over seemingly small things.

It has mostly been his unwillingness to accept that I had the gravitas to tell him what to do, better known in parenting, as a test of wills. It was an interesting dynamic between us, especially as he got older and became a teenager. I know other mothers raising teen boys, without their father, have had a lot to contend with too. I must admit that my circumstance seemed unique to me, even if it was one of my own making.

After my divorce, I kept Doc away from Mele. Hawaii was one of the first states to allow women who divorced to take back their maiden name. If they had custody of the children, they could change their names as well. This is what I did. Protecting Mele and earning money became my main priorities, out of necessity.

When my business career took off, I put him in private Christian school. It was my belief at the time that a good Christian education would serve him well in the long run. It took me a long time to realize that there was a lot of prejudice and backwards thinking in some of these schools. Their methodology was more indoctrination and not really education. He did not go to public school until high school and by that time he was chomping at the bit with resentments.

We moved to Florida to be closer to family and for my business career. His high school years were difficult for us both. Aunt Lee moved in with us and she did all she could to help. She drove him to school almost every day and anywhere else he needed to go. She did all the housework for me and cooked great meals for us. She kept us in order. She was elderly by this time, and it was a lot of work for her. Soon after Mele graduated from high school, she decided to move to live near her youngest brother, Lang, who was her last remaining sibling left alive. They were both well up in their eighties by then and I was getting ready to marry Pete, so it seemed like a good thing for all of us. I really loved all my aunts, but Aunt Lee and I had a special bond.

She had given me and Mele so much love that it was difficult to see her leave our home that she had really created by filling in whenever my work kept me away or I was too busy to attend to things on the home front. She paid close attention to everything and gave us a sense of security that made it possible for my career success. The spiritual advice that she gave us was invaluable. She was a great woman of faith. That really seemed to help Mele, even in his rebellious teens. Aunt Lee was very empathetic to him because she said that she had been a rebellious and hardheaded teenager, too.

Once Mele started college, I thought I was out of the woods with him. He had a part-time job at the daily newspaper under a protégé' of mine, his own off campus apartment, and a car. Since Pete lived in a rented bachelor apartment and I owned a four bedroom, three bath family home that was now empty except for me, he moved into my house. As newlyweds, we were enjoying our newfound love nest which we redecorated to suit our mutual taste and needs. The next thing we know, I get a call from my friend at the newspaper to tell me he's so disappointed that Mel is leaving the job because he is a talented graphics artist which was what he was studying in college.

Needless to say, that we hurriedly set up a lunch date with Mele, who informed us that he had joined the Marines and was getting married. We immediately thought there must be a pregnancy involved. Pete asked him how far along was the pregnancy. Mele went off on us with such anger that we were stunned into silence. Before we could get any further information, he stormed out of the restaurant in the middle of the meal.

Pete had never seen that side of him, nor was he ever able to un-see it. From that day on, even though, he supported me in my "odd odyssey" with Mele, he has never trusted him, nor allowed him to get close to him emotionally. He handles him like he's a wild card that could cause havoc at any moment. They try to do things together and get along for my sake, but Pete is wary when Mele is present, like he's watching a cobra. I knew the feeling because I'd been there with Wick at one time so what could I do to change the dynamics but ignore the elephant in the room – hard feelings.

The four of us ate dinner together in relative peace and Mele said he would like to take Momma to the airport in Sacramento, but Pete and I were ahead of him because we had her leaving out of Redding. If he took her there, he could go on straight back to the program center in Cottonwood. He knew we were a couple of steps ahead of him because we'd dealt with his devious behavior before. We'd learned how to corral it by basically, out planning him. There was no way that we would sanction him going into the city when his pass was only for coming here. The program had restrictions for a reason. He knew the temptations of street drug life would be too much for him to resist in Sacramento. The fact that he tried it put a damper on the evening. We all retired early with the excuse that Momma needed to pack and get herself ready for the long trip to Florida. As we often do when Mele is with us, Pete and I talked into the night about our opinion of his mental, emotional, and physical health.

Pete's take was that he seemed to be bidding his time until he could get back into his addiction lifestyle. I saw what he saw but tried to put a different spin on it. I thought that more time at the ranch would make a difference in his attitude. He'd told us that he enjoyed the physical work that the rehab ranch required. He was clearing a field for cattle, and he excitedly told us about a rattlesnake nest that he'd come across. He'd captured all the rattlesnakes and now had this idea to turn Joyland into a rattlesnake farm. He said caring for these reptiles assured a constant source of valuable venom for making the serum. He also enthusiastically explained that a live rattlesnake was worth a couple hundred dollars. I told him that I was not going to live on a rattle snake farm.

I thought about the huge snake that had crossed the driveway in front of my truck not that long ago and told him about it. I told him this place already had enough rattlers and to carry out that dreadful idea somewhere else.

He just laughed loudly, like some evil genius or more like Wick, and said, "I know that, Mom, but it really is a good idea."

His childhood years had been spent in Hawaii, which has no snakes, thanks to the Mongoose, so he has no fear of these dangerous reptiles. These are the kind of odd things that he never grew out of. Mele once talked to me about his experience with the Marines, where they sent them into Bangladesh after a severe cyclonic storm, with huge tidal surges that flooded the coastal areas of the country. Thousands were killed and property worth billions of dollars was destroyed. He said that they had to load the supplies onto smaller boats because the harbor and docking stations were destroyed, and the big ship couldn't get close. When the smaller boats got close to shore, they still had to unload their cargo and wade in the chest high debris-filled water with the supply containers over their heads. The water was also filled with snakes. Unlike Mele, some guys were just frozen with fear and couldn't do it. Mele's boat was unloaded first. Then they started helping other boats unload their cargo. I asked him how he did it and he said he prayed with his crew and released them from the "Fear of the Serpent". Some of the guys had been in one of the middle eastern wars together and they trusted each other. None of his guys were attacked by snakes even when some of the locals were bitten. I thought it was miraculous, but he said his faith just kicked up a notch. However, some of his guys had nightmares all the way to the Philippines, where they were sent for R&R.

Mele also has an affinity for odd and strange people. This was another thing that had led to his twisted path and strange bedfellows, especially since he'd left the military. This has caused me a lot of consternation because when I talk to Mele, he sees my point about his choices, but he seems unable to make changes. Although he's a grown man, his actions still have consequences for me and the family. I feel an obligation to give my parental advice even if it seems to fall on deaf ears until he runs into the inevitable trouble.

Joanie called me early morning to let me know that she was back home. The wildfire had been brought under control without any lost of structure or life. She reported that the mop up operation was almost complete and about 5,000 acres were burned. She said she anticipated the operation would be de-mobilizing within the next 24 hours. I mentioned that Mele was visiting. She said she'd let Carpenter know because those two 'oddballs' were friends. They kind of thought alike. I hadn't told him about Carpenter's newfound fortune because I considered it a personal matter. Before we finished our coffee, Chez was barking a greeting up the hill where Mele's trailer was situated. I heard Carpenter's old truck pulling into the trailer driveway. Chez had spent the night up there and hadn't come back for her breakfast. Pete had put some items of food in the little fridge up there. They were probably eating those things. The trailer was stocked with plastic containers of coffee, sugar and basics. Mele fed Chez whatever he ate, and she loved that.

I saw the three of them walking down our driveway, Chez, Mele and Carpenter. Oh boy, I chuckled to myself, they seem to have something on their minds. Momma had her things packed except for what she planned to wear for travel and was in the kitchen. Pete was in the powerhouse checking the generator because it had run part of the night. Mele leaves his TV on all night, no matter how many times we remind him that we electrify off a solar system primarily. Anyway, I came down from my office nook and came out on the deck to greet them. Chez, the traitor, tried to act like she had not abandoned me for her favorite person and danced around me for minute until she realized that I was going to ignore her, as her punishment. Finally, she sat down with a sigh in her favorite spot. I offered coffee and they both accepted. Momma said she would bring out a tray. We went around to the back deck and sat at the table. Pete came out of the powerhouse and joined us. He already had a large mug of coffee in his hand.

Carpenter started the conversation with, "You know I've been looking for investment ideas now that I have some extra cash coming to me. I like Mele's idea of a rattlesnake farm. That guy from Cornell is trying to sell his underground place up on Chrome Mine Road. He's getting married and moving back east where his fiancé lives. Have you been inside that place? It's dug into the mountainside on his land and the inside is amazing. The guy studied experimental design at Cornell. Cornell University is home to one of the oldest and most respected architecture programs in the United States. Clearly, he learned a lot. This place would make a great facility for what we want. His price is reasonable because he is a motivated seller.   You know, I can pay cash."

He looked at Pete to see what he thought because Pete also worked for the Small Business Administration giving workshops to small and micro business startups on how to write a business plan and get financing from SBA. Pete is an early bird and he'd already been on his computer this morning, looking up snake farming because he always like to be informed when he spoke on anything with Mele. Information kept down arguments and he liked to come with the facts. He also knew that Mele was a bulldog when it came to any of his harebrained ideas like panning for gold, as a money-making career. He'd bought a washed out claim with some of his military disability money and of course that had not worked out to be profitable.

Pete said, "You need to know that there's a good reason only two laboratories in the US produce pretty much all the venom used for research and anti-venom production. To do this, you need a sizeable facility for breeding and maintaining captive snakes, a customized environment for handling them and collecting the venom, the equipment to immediately lyophilize ("freeze-dry") the collected venom, a laboratory for analyzing the venom for purity, tremendous safety precautions, a ton of regulatory permits, etc. THEN, you'd have to arrange contracts with anti-venom producers and/or research facilities to have a market—which means you'd have to out-compete the existing players in the industry who've had established contracts for many years. Venom producers must adhere to very stringent requirements established by their customers, and in order to avoid overnight bankruptcy, you'd have to have committed orders for all your production before extraction ever began. To be honest, it's a very, very difficult market to penetrate and would require a huge investment in facility and equipment up- front. I couldn't advise anyone to even consider it without first having developed a committed customer base.

Harvesting skins is an entirely different issue and I'm not sure about the legality of that. I suspect it is dependent on location because many laws regulating wildlife are specific to the state or county level. With either enterprise, it would be necessary to research all the legal issues well in advance, because many locales would prevent you from housing a large number of live venomous snakes, and others would prohibit their slaughter. It goes without saying, of course, that it would be illegal to remove animals from the wild for either purpose, so they'd have to be captive bred, which means you would need personnel with experience in that area, too. Now, there might be a market for the meat because I see folks selling it online."

None of what Pete said seemed to deter Carpenter and Mele. The guys and Chez went off gleefully to look at the "laboratory", which apparently is what they were now calling the supped-up cave house. Pete and I sat there for awhile stunned. Momma came back out and we told her what was going on. The three of us were laughing. I reminded them about the premonition that I'd shared when I saw the huge rattler not that long ago. Pete said if they started that farm, we'd have to move because it would get too wild west for him. He said, 'No Country for Old Men', referring to a novel that we had both read that was going to be a movie soon.

I decided to call Joanie and give her a heads up with the prayer that she could talk Carpenter out of the crazy venture. To my surprise she started laughing like a mad woman and said, "T h a t money is already burning a hole in his pocket. He hasn't gotten the deposit into his account yet. Now he's going around like he's a big-time entrepreneur. Hope, I'll do my best to get him to change his mind, but you know what he's like. Now we could try to make up some sort of regulation on something like this for the district and try to get the County Supervisors to pass it. That takes time. He probably wouldn't care if they made it illegal anyway. He and Mele would just put-up fences and signs. Who would want to come and have a shoot-out with rattlesnake ranglers." She howled laughing again as she hung up the phone.

I shook my head at Pete and Momma and told them what Joanie said. We had no paddle up this murky creek, and we knew it. After a lifetime of dealing with Mele, I felt exhausted and defeated because I was certain that Pete and I would move away from my wonderful sanctuary, Joyland, because of him. I went up stairs and laid down across the bed. I was tired of the responsibility of motherhood.   My child was too old for me to deal with his side winding ways. No matter what, Mele always found a way to get what he wanted from me, even if he had to destroy something in my life. Perhaps, that wasn't fair. I have felt that way too often with him and right now I was having trouble dealing with it. I also knew from experience that once he was out of my presence for a while, I'd change my mind and want to see, hug, and talk to him. That seemed to be my lot in life with this soul who came to me in the strangest way and who I loved with all my being. It has always been a journey of hopefulness through all the trials (literally or figuratively) and tribulations. I must 'keep hope alive' to quote a famous preacher and civil rights icon.

The next morning, he put all of Momma's luggage in his Bronco. The two of them piled in the car, while Chez danced anxiously around because she knew they were leaving. She loved them both and would clearly miss them. As they pulled the vehicle around the circular drive, Pete and I stood with arms around each other and waved goodbye to the other two folks that I loved the most in the world. Both were often difficult for me to deal with. They both shaped, sharpened, and polished me like only diamond-bladed edges could. If I really thought about it, I felt lucky to have them in my life and on this journey with me. Love never dies. That is just the way it is, no matter what else happens or how it happens.

"Love you, Momma!" Mele and I shouted at the same time.

THE END

Afterwards - About the Author

Often we read a book and wonder about the person who wrote it but we find very little insight or info about the author except perhaps where they reside or with whom. This author wants to share a little more with the readers about her personal path and journey through life's winding roads.   Included are some photographs of her and the people she has loved along the way – just some snapshots of moments in her timeline.

Ingrid Landis-Davis

This book is fictional and some of the characters are composites of folks that have brought their interesting personalities and experiences into the author's circle of life.

Some of the settings are historical and some of the story lines are taken from real occurrences. The author has drawn the novel's idea from family stories and personal experiences but this is a work of fiction created from her active imagination and natural tendency to write and talk history. She has been to and lived in all the places that she describes so that part is not fictitious. This author has served as a businesswoman, media and social influencer, fire chief, government official, community and political organizer, environmental conservationist, wife, single mom, and other roles that life has brought to her. She hopes you've enjoyed this journey as much as she has loved sharing it with you.

Ingrid Landis-Davis has published a novel, *Short Side of the Triangle*; a cookbook, *Exotic Soul Kitchen*; and a poetry collection, *Blues Child's~Verse to Song*.   She has extensive nonprofit, corporate and community outreach experience, including an excellent background in publishing, media, editing, grant writing, grant administration, public relations and public speaking.

Musical References

Keys to the Highway (BB Bronzy, C. Segal, J. Gillum);
Walking Blues (Robert Johnson);
You Can't Hurry God (as performed by Mahalia Jackson)
Friends in Low Places (performed by Garth Brooks);
Pu'uanahulu (Gabby Pahinui);
Ipo Lei Manu (Queen Kapiolani);
You Don't Know What Love Is (D. Raye, G. de Paul);
You Can Have Him (Irving Berlin);
Gonna Move Up To The Country-Paint My Mailbox Blue (Taj Mahal);
Going Up Country (A. Wilson, B. White, Canned Heat);
Easy To Love Man (Ingrid L-D);
Bill Came Through (Ingrid L-D);
Country Roads (John Denver)
I'm A Man (Bo Diddley)
I Shall Be Released (Bob Dylan)

Endnotes

1 John 14:2; Hebrews 12:1 (King James Bible)

2 Hermeneutics is the science and the art of biblical interpretation. It is a science because there are rules for interpreting Scripture, just as there are rules for driving a car. If you do not know the rules, you will not know how to drive properly. Beyond knowing the principles, however, you must also know when to apply them. Because of this, hermeneutics can also rightly be called an art.

3 Sephardic or Sephardi Jews Jewry of Hispania; Ladino: also Sephardim or Peninsular Jews are a Jewish diaspora population associated with the Iberian Peninsula. The term is derived from the Hebrew Sepharad can also refer to the Mizrahi Jews of Western Asia and North Africa, who were also influenced by Sephardic law and custom. Many Iberian Jewish exiles also later sought refuge in Mizrahi Jewish communities, resulting in integration with those communities.

4 The Rootless Root (*Blues Child's Verse to Song* by Ingrid Landis-Davis).

Reference books:
Thunder Up The Creek by Claude A. "Herk" Shriner
Buffalo Soldiers In The West – A Black Soldiers Anthology Edited by Bruce A. Glasrud and Michael N. Searles
Buffalo Soldiers – A Narrative of the Black Cavalry in the West by William H, Leckie with Shirley A. Leckie

Photo credits:
Cover photo-Flickr.com- Leading to Sunset -Marvin Kurti
Page 12 - iStockphoto.com -180726936 Chief
Page 26 - iStockphoto.com Volcano Essentials 1023671946
Credit: Jim Wiltschko

Acknowledgements and Thanks

Captain Paul Matthews, Archivist and Founder of the Buffalo Soldiers National Museum in Houston, TX
Hardie Grove Baptist Church, Oxford, NC
Trinity County Fire Chiefs Association, Weaverville, CA
Roberta Kapalili and G. 'Smitty' Smith, Docents at Hulihe'e Palace in Kailua-Kona, HI

Finally, I want to thank my friends and family for their unwavering love, support, encouragement, understanding and prayers. My editor, Ersula K. Odom of Sula Too Publishing has had my back every step in this process and I could not have finished this novel without her emotional and intuitive intelligence.

Paul Davis, the great man that I'm married to, has been with me through all the twists and turns of writing this book. Paul's good natured humor, care and love sustained me through this patchwork journey.

With Much Love and Mahalo,
Ingrid